The steaming water is an anesthesia. I stand under it for a long time trying to relax. Wondering what will happen with Kate. Clearly, after all the time we've spent together in the past weeks, the shared chemistry between us is growing. Stepping out of the shower, I reach for a towel on the stool next to the sink. But someone's hand is already on it. I feel the towel brush across my back and over my shoulders. Just behind me, I hear the words as they are softly spoken. "Turn around and look at me."

I turn and look into Kate's eyes, the one place I should never have looked to find escape, but where I might look to find steadiness, strength. I square my jaw to the fluttering sensations in my stomach, the water dripping from my hair into my eyes.

"Are you as scared as I am?" I ask her, beginning to shiver.

Kate takes me into her arms. "No, but I'll pretend."

We fall onto the bed. Kate's still dressed. Her hands are on my breasts, lips kissing my neck. Slowly, I unbutton her blouse, run my tongue across her bra — feel the hard nipples underneath. Kate looks down and smiles, removing the rest of her clothes.

About the Author

Laura DeHart Young has been a writer and editor of business publications for the past ten years. She lives in Reading, Pennsylvania with her partner of seven years, two Pugs and three felines. She is currently at work on her second novel.

There Will Be No Goodbyes

LAURA DEHART YOUNG

THE NAIAD PRESS, INC.
1995

Printed in the United States of America on acid-free paper
First Edition

Edited by Christine Cassidy
Cover design by Bonnie Liss (Phoenix Graphics)
Typeset by Sandi Stancil

Library of Congress Cataloging-in-Publication Data

Young, Laura DeHart, 1956 –
    There will be no goodbyes / by Laura DeHart Young.
        p.   cm.
    ISBN 1-56280-103-1
    I. Title.
PS3575.0799T48   1995
813'.54—dc20   94-43818
                                                            CIP

For Jan.
There is a room in my heart
filled with you.

Acknowledgments

I would like to thank my dear friends Susan Moran and Lori Trezise for their loving support and encouragement.

CHAPTER ONE

It's early September in Vienna, Virginia. For a moment, I stop to gaze at the open fields beyond the fence bordering the farm. The land seems to welcome the change of seasons. There is a chill in the evening air I hadn't noticed before, and other changes in the landscape I might've recognized in years past. But the passage of time has taken on a new meaning — no longer marked solely by changes in the weather.

The packages I hold are suddenly heavy, making me move toward the house. As I open the back door, the dog is there to greet me. I pet her, stroking her soft fur. "So, how's Mom today? Let's go check."

The dog follows me to the bottom of the living room steps. I hesitate, not wanting to wake Chris. Then I hear a rustling sound upstairs.

"Chris, you awake?"

"I'm awake."

"Just stopped by with the groceries you needed. You hungry?"

"Not really."

"How 'bout a salad and some fruit?"

"No, I'm really not hungry."

"Can I come up?"

"Please do."

After putting the groceries away, I grab the *Washington Post* and start upstairs, Maggie following at my heels. At the top of the steps I trip, almost landing flat on my face. "Who turned out the lights?" I ask, trying to regain my balance.

"Sorry. I was sitting here in the dark waiting for you."

"Can I turn on the light?"

"Okay."

I feel for the switch, flipping it on with the palm of my hand. "There, now you can gaze upon my beauty."

Today I get a smile from her. She's sitting up, pillows propped behind her. She looks pale and tired. I push those thoughts away.

"Brought the paper."

"Thanks. What would I do without you, Buddie? Guess I'd be in bigger trouble than I already am."

"I'll be here as long as you need me."

Chris yawns. "I'm really tired. Think I'll take a nap."

"Maggie needs a walk. We'll go for a quick one, then I'll lock up for you." I flick the light switch off again.

"Buddie, before you leave, can I ask a favor? Will you stay and hold me for a while?"

I stop in the doorway, turning to look at her — a soft shadow in the darkness. In the moonlight I see the outline of her small frame, hunched over, trembling. Without saying anything, I sit down on the edge of the bed. When I feel her hand touch my shoulder, I take her gently into my arms; she seems so frail and small.

"I'm scared," she says, resting her head on my shoulder.

"So am I."

I hold her like that for hours that seem like moments. A thousand thoughts assault me, of what life might be like without Chris. It had been six months since Chris had found out about her heart condition. Cardiomyopathy. The cumbersome word sticks in my brain. A degenerative disease that destroys the heart muscle. The doctor told Chris it had probably been caused by a virus that attacked her heart. She could live six months. She could live six years. Could live? Could die. Thoughts of living without Chris bring a stinging emptiness — the same emptiness I had felt as a child, not yet six. My father was dead of cancer at the age of thirty-two. Gone. The image of a man faded with time. What kind of man had he been?

I leave the room as Chris lies sleeping. Sitting for

the rest of the night on the downstairs sofa, I stare into the blackness. The anger, the pain, the confusion are all there, swirling like autumn leaves on a windy day. I can't sort through my thoughts fast enough to make sense of anything, too empty to know how to cope. I pray that I can put my emotions and doubts aside to be strong for her.

From my office window at radio stations WASH-FM and AM, I have an excellent view of the Old Downtown section of Washington, D.C. Daydreaming, I watch the hustle and bustle of 9th street. Not far away is the White House, the F.B.I. Building, Ford's Theatre and the National Archives. It feels like the center of everything happening in this city — and an ideal location if you happen to be a news reporter.

The extension in my office rings and I pick it up.

"Buddie, it's Harry. Stop by to see me before you leave."

Hearing the name "Buddie," I laugh silently. Even my boss has picked up on the childhood nickname.

Harold Taylor, general manager of both radio stations, is on the phone when I arrive. He motions me in and I take the seat in front of his desk. Dressed in an expensive gray suit, he's leaning back in his chair. He talks in a loud, booming voice while clipping his fingernails — tiny pieces of nail landing in various locations across the large desk.

Fifteen minutes later, Harry ends the conversation, slamming the phone down in the professional manner to which I've grown accustomed.

"Buddie, how are you?" he says beaming. He places the nail clippers in the top right drawer of his desk. I wonder what other things he keeps in that drawer.

"Fine, Harry. What can I do for you?"

"You're covering the rally tomorrow at the Mall."

"The rally for AIDS research funding? Yes, I am."

"There will be live reports, I assume."

"Of course."

Not one to mince words, Harry gets right to the point of our meeting. "I want to caution you on any live interviews. Let's be prudent when it comes to on-air remarks. I don't want to hear a lot of radical homosexuals screaming about how rotten the government and this country have been to them. If remarks are calmly made, and backed up with facts, fine. But if you've got to do some creative editing in the studio, then do it."

"I don't anticipate any problems, Harry. The National Gay and Lesbian Task Force, sponsor of the rally, is a very reputable organization. I don't think I'd call them radicals."

"Buddie, you're an excellent reporter. But let's not get caught up in idealistic fantasies. We've got a lot of good sponsors and advertisers we can't afford to piss off. Are we understanding each other?"

"Yes, but I think you have a misconception of who these people are. They're confronting some serious issues. Lack of funding for AIDS research is a reality."

"No doubt. But as I said, if there are any problems, the story's going to get buried at the end of a five minute newscast."

"That won't be necessary."

"Good. One more thing. Take Doug with you. He's new and needs the experience."

I nod and get up. As I exit Harry's office, a stream of less than prudent thoughts flies through my head. Without a single mental edit, I let them fly.

The Mall, located in between the Capitol and the Washington Monument, is swarming with thousands of people. Press passes in hand, Doug and I make our way to the section up front which has been roped off for reporters. In between his grumblings, Doug sets up the remote broadcasting equipment.

"Need some help?" I offer, bending down next to him.

"No. I can't believe I had to give up my Saturday to record a bunch of queers."

"I'll try to forget I heard that remark."

"Why should you care?"

"We're reporters. We're supposed to be objective."

Doug stares at me, his dark eyes shifting up and down. Then he laughs, a sickening kind of laugh that goes right through me. "I thought there was something funny about you," he says with disgust. "You're one of them, aren't you?"

I feel myself turning red — not out of shame, but of anger. "That's none of your business. We're here to do a job."

"Guess that answers my question," he says, shaking his head. "And I thought being here was bad enough. Now I've got to work with one."

"I'm not interested in what you think, now or ever. We're here to cover this rally whether you like it or not. I'm going to get a couple of interviews before this thing gets underway. Stay here with the rest of the equipment."

"Don't worry, I'm not going anywhere."

Behind the podium and stage area I find a group of National Gay and Lesbian Task Force officials. I gravitate toward two women, clipboards in hand, engaged in a vigorous conversation.

"Excuse me, I'm Liz Callow from WASH-FM. I'd like to get an interview from an NGLTF representative on today's activities."

The women eye my press badge, then escort me about five yards to my right where a group of people are congregated.

"You'll want to talk to Kathryn McGowan. She's in charge of p.r., and one of the organizers of today's rally. Hang around. I'll get her for you."

While waiting, I check my equipment to make sure it works. Placing a new tape inside the recorder, I test the record levels, readjusting them slightly.

A few moments later, I notice a short, slim woman walking in my direction. In addition to a red ribbon pin, she's wearing a button that says simply, "Research Funding for AIDS."

"Hi, Kate McGowan. I understand you'd like an interview."

"Yes, I'm Liz Callow from WASH-FM. I only need to ask a few questions."

"Shoot," she answers, folding her arms in front of her.

Turning on the microphone, I look up at the woman standing in front of me. She's disarming, her face strikingly beautiful. Suddenly I'm nervous.

"Do you believe that funding for AIDS research is keeping pace with the spread of the disease?"

"Absolutely not. That's what this rally is all about. We need to raise the level of AIDS funding, and we need to do it now. Research into new drugs, prevention, treatment and a cure has to be given a higher priority."

As she talks, I can't help noticing her strength and confidence. I follow the movement of her hands as she speaks with a directness and knowledge that's impressive.

"We need to see more community-based AIDS services dedicated to prevention, counseling, diagnosis and other health-related issues. AIDS-designated care centers are still needed in the major cities throughout the country to cope with the rising number of new patients and to purchase and administer AZT."

"There's been an increase in funding, particularly federal, in the past two years, correct?"

Probably in her late thirties, I think, noticing the lines around her eyes and mouth. At five feet eight-inches, I'm several inches taller than she is, but her slight build in no way diminishes the strength of her presence.

"Yes, that's true. But with the first Republican congress in 50 years, we're fearful of cut-backs."

"We have an AIDS Czar — and big p.r. events like World AIDS Day. Are these changes helping?

"On the surface in terms of general awareness. But some of this stuff isn't very meaningful in terms of solid results."

"What do you hope will be accomplished by today's rally?"

I notice her eyes — the color of rich, brown earth. Her hair falls softly in hues of auburn and blonde.

"To impress upon the public, that although we've made some moves in the right direction regarding funding, we still have a long way to go. This is a disease that's already claimed more lives than the Korean War, Vietnam War and Desert Storm combined. We need more fully-funded health studies and programs that'll finally put an end to the dying."

I turn off the recorder, signaling the end of the interview. "Thanks for your time."

"Will this be broadcast tonight?"

"During the six o'clock newscast."

The woman extends her hand and I take it. "Look forward to hearing it. I listen to your station all the time. Just moved here from New York. It'll be nice to hear a familiar voice on my way home from work."

Two hours of editing later, the story is ready for the evening newscast. The final version seems anti-climactic, but includes the strong, eloquent words of Kathryn McGowan. I'm certain hers is a voice I'll hear again.

When I arrive at Chris's farm it's quiet and peaceful, the darkness of the evening a blanket over the house and the field. A cool breeze blows across the openness, stinging my face — the edge of it biting as September fades into autumn.

I fumble at the door with my keys, finally getting it open. The living room is quiet and dark until I hear the clicking of the dog's toenails. Maggie greets me excitedly, licking my face, her front legs on top of my shoulders.

"Were you a good girl today? Did you take care of your mother?"

Draping my coat over the living room chair, I make my way to the kitchen. It looks as though Chris has eaten, so I wash the dishes, take Maggie for a walk and then settle myself on the sofa. I only intend to rest a few minutes before checking on Chris, but I fall asleep.

. . . I open the door to my parents' house and it's quiet inside. Until I hear the sounds of sobbing coming from the first-floor bedroom. Even though I'm frightened, I move toward the sounds — creeping around the corner to the open door. Inside the room my brother, Tom, has his face buried in a pillow at the foot of my parents' bed. My mother is sitting next to him, stroking the back of his head. I try not to be noticed, struggling to figure out what's wrong. And then, as if from instinct, my mother senses my presence in the doorway. As she looks at me, her face stained with tears, I feel my stomach pulling and knotting with fear. I'm afraid to see her cry, to see my brother, who's always bigger and braver than I am, cry.

"Buddie, come here," my mother says, reaching for me. But my feet are heavy and stuck to the floor. My brother turns to me, eyes wet, nose dripping. Pulling the sleeve of his shirt over his crumpled fist, he wipes away the newest tears, but not the horror; it stays on his face, creeping across the room into my heart. Somehow, he gets out the words I could never have said.

"Elizabeth, Daddy's dead."

I look at him as the room closes in, the light gone suddenly dim and dark. He's lying, I think, my feet still stuck to the floor. He's always playing games. Always telling stories.

My mother moves to the edge of the bed, clutching the bedspread. "Buddie, do you know what it means to die?"

"No," I lie, hoping they will think I'm too dumb to bother explaining.

"It means you go to heaven to be with God."

I glare at my mother. She's lying too. When you die they put you in a hole in the ground, and you never see the person again. Yes, they both think I'm dumb. Why else would I be sticking to the floor?

My mother reaches out to me, finally able to grab an arm and pull me to her. She strokes my head as the lump in my throat threatens to choke me, my brother's sobs mixing with my own . . .

I wake up to a sensation of warmth on my head. In the dim light of the living room I think I see my mother, but it's Chris standing over me, stroking my head as though I'm a child. As she bends over me, she looks concerned, her small frame silhouetted against the desk light.

"Sorry, didn't mean to wake you. Rough day for you. You must be exhausted." She sits down next to the couch in a lotus position, arms wrapped around her knees. "I listened to you on the radio tonight. You did a great job. The rally must've been interesting."

"It was. How was your day?"

"I feel better."

I notice how thin she's become from the neck down. In sharp contrast is the puffiness of her face, the result of large doses of steroids. But she's still beautiful to me — her shoulder-length dark hair catching the room's light, framing a soft and gentle face. From the couch, I reach down and hold the first three fingers of her right hand. Chris looks up and smiles.

"Hope I can get back to the shop next week. Jean called today. The framing orders are piling up. And I've got several paintings to finish for the museum show next month."

"Everything will be fine."

"I know."

"I better get going. What time is it?"

"After eleven o'clock. You might as well stay here tonight. It's late and you're tired."

"Well, I am a little bleary-eyed."

Letting go of my hand, Chris stands up. "And I won't have you sleeping on this couch, either. Sitting on it's bad enough. I always save it for the guests I don't like."

"Is that why I always end up on it?"

12

"Very funny. Come upstairs."

"Do you have a T-shirt or something I can wear? One that could possibly fit this heavenly body?"

She laughs. "I think I can manage it. Bob left some old shirts here."

"Do you still hear from him?" I ask tentatively.

"He called today. Hadn't talked to him in a while. It was hard hearing his voice."

Silently, I wish I had Bob's address. Even though I've never met him, I have the urge to kill him. One day, almost two years ago, he'd walked into Chris's shop. He was married with two children but, by the time Chris found out, she was already in love with him. The relationship continued until she became ill. Then he hit her with the news. He loved her but couldn't leave his wife. He couldn't bear the thought of hurting his children. They agreed, after that discussion, not to see each other again. At the time, I thought Chris had taken the news well. But I know better now. She was devastated; she really needed him. I imagine kicking him where it hurts the most.

In bed, thoughts of Chris alone and needing someone gnaw at me.

"Do you think you'll ever see him again?" I ask.

"I don't think so."

"I'm sorry. I know you need someone now."

"Not really. I have you, my dearest friend. It's more than I could've asked for."

Chris touches the left side of my face, a delicate stroke that comes and goes before I have time to react. She turns away and so do I, exhausted and barely able to keep my eyes open. The thought of her next to me lingers, until finally I fall asleep. Early in the morning when I wake up, her arm is resting lightly across my waist, head nestled against my back. Thoughts of killing Bob resurface then fade again as I place my arms across hers. Maybe this is better. I know I'll never hurt her.

As I stare, the pile of work on my desk stares back. A half an hour passes and, although I've shuffled through some papers here and there, I've accomplished nothing. Then the phone rings and I'm saved once again from having to think.

"Liz Callow, can I help you?"

"Liz, Kate McGowan. You interviewed me at the rally last Saturday. I wanted to call and thank you for the excellent coverage the station provided. Your efforts were greatly appreciated."

"That's nice to hear."

"I also wanted to invite you to a party I'm having this weekend. I'd like to introduce you to some people who are active in the task force. It's not all business, of course. I thought you might be interested."

"When is it?"

"This Friday at eight. Think you can make it?"

"I think so."

"Terrific. I'll call you Friday with directions. Have a great week."

After hanging up the phone, I notice my hands are perspiring. I have no idea why.

CHAPTER TWO

That Friday, while washing dishes after dinner, I
stare out the back window in Chris's kitchen. Night
has fallen over the nearby field, and lustrous stars
form a pattern above browning grasses. A vacant
space inside me wishes this evening were over and
that sleep, like a still field, would take my mind off
the present.

"Going out tonight?"

I turn, pulling my hands from the hot water.
Chris is sitting at the kitchen table, stroking Maggie's
butterscotch fur.

"I've been invited to a party."

"You're dripping."

Suds have pooled on the kitchen floor. Shaking my hands over the sink, I grab a paper towel to wipe the spill.

"Who's giving the party?" Chris asks as I bend down to clean the floor.

"The woman I interviewed at the Mall last Saturday. One of the organizers of the AIDS rally."

"It was nice of her to invite you. I mean, you only met her once."

"It was nice."

"You don't seem too excited."

I unplug the drain and dry my hands. "How excited can I be? I won't know a single soul there."

"You'll know her."

"I met Kathryn once for about fifteen minutes. That hardly qualifies as knowing someone."

"She obviously thinks it qualifies."

"Well, she seems a little more outgoing than I am."

"If you feel uncomfortable, why go?"

I sit down at the kitchen table, taking the chair across from Chris. She looks at me with a funny half-smile, her deep brown eyes dull and tired.

"Something tells me I should. Meeting new people might be good for me."

"Well, we know I'm not going to be around forever. So you should make new friends."

I glance at Chris but she looks away, petting the dog as though the stinging comment had never been made.

"That's a hell of a thing to say."

"It's the truth."

"Look, you could stand getting out of the house, too. Why don't you come along?"

"No, I'm worse than you in a crowd full of strangers. Go and have fun. I've got a good book to read."

Chris gets up abruptly. In the living room, she turns on the stereo. I follow her, sensing a discomfort I don't want to leave with. "Maybe I should stay here so we can talk."

"Talk about what?" she asks with her back toward me.

"You and me. What we're feeling."

"I know what I'm feeling. There's no point discussing it."

"Yes, there is." I put my hand on her shoulder. "There is a point to it. Maybe I need to hear what you're thinking. I don't want you to shut me out."

Chris looks at me. Her eyes are as pain-filled as I've ever seen them. "Go to the party, Buddie. I need some time to be alone."

"If anything were ever to happen to you, life wouldn't just go on. You must know that."

"What are you going to do, Buddie? Come with me?"

"Damnit, isn't it hard enough without this kind of talk?"

"Hard for who, Buddie? How the hell do you think I feel? I'm the one who's dying here!"

"So that's it. You're just going to give up! Look, I know you've been through a lot in the last six months . . ."

"Buddie, you don't know anything! I get weaker every day. I feel like shit! And I'm not in the mood for your naive optimism."

Chris pushes me aside and goes back into the kitchen. Again, I'm right behind her. She's leaning over the sink, tears running down her face. I put my arms around her from behind, kiss her lightly on the neck. She jumps, then moves away.

"Back off, Buddie. Don't do this to me now. Go to your fucking party and leave me alone! I've got some serious dying to do here."

I feel a door slam in my face, a door I hadn't wanted to open in the first place. I grab my coat and head for the car, sure I've lost my mind along with any sense that may have come with it.

"I don't believe we've met," says the young woman who opens the door. As she takes my coat, I introduce myself. "Are you a friend of Kate's?" she asks.

"I've only met her once."

"Well, enjoy the party. The bar's in the kitchen, so help yourself.

At the other end of the room Kathryn, with great animation, is telling a story. I don't hear what she's saying, but it must be funny because people are laughing out loud and finding it difficult to remain in their seats.

I take a beer from the refrigerator, noticing again how beautiful Kathryn is. Her strong, Irish face and dark brown eyes complement a breathtaking smile.

Finally, her story finished, Kathryn looks up and sees me. That same smile crosses her face, changing the hue of her eyes. She puts her drink down and walks over to me.

18

"Liz, really glad you could join us. Hey, this is Liz Callow — world famous news announcer," she says.

"Is this the one you've been talking about?" asks a woman to my left.

"You bet. Liz is a reporter for WASH-FM. Last weekend she covered the rally. It was a terrific story." Kathryn puts her arm around my shoulder, leading me into the crowded living room. "I'm really glad you came," she says, sitting down on the arm of the nearest sofa. "Are you comfortable?"

"I don't know anyone. But I'll survive."

"A nice-looking group of women if I do say so myself."

"I always like being in a room full of lovely and interesting women."

"As soon as you asked your first question on Saturday, I knew you were one of us. It was something in your voice."

"If that's the case, all of D.C. knows."

"Hey, we need strong voices in important places. C'mon, I'll show you the rest of the house."

After the house tour, Kathryn and I end up on an enclosed porch. Tables have been arranged to accommodate the overflow of people, but no one seems to have noticed. Shimmering candles, set in the middle of each table, create a serene effect I welcome.

"Sit down. We can watch the stars together," Kathryn says with a wink. She rests her hand on my shoulder. "I'll get a couple of beers and be right back. Don't go away."

When Kathryn returns, she sits across the table, close enough for me to really see her, to notice her expressions, reactions, idiosyncrasies. She begins to talk about her past. I watch her intently, the evening shadows adding a distracting intimacy to the conversation.

"Living in New York City was crazy. I was mugged twice. By the time I left, I had so many stray cats coming to my door, I could barely afford to feed them all." As she speaks, she leans her chin into her left hand, crosses and uncrosses her legs.

"How long did you live there?"

"Two years, three months and nine days."

"I get the point."

"I've lived in Washington for a year now. I'm originally from California. Ever been out there?"

"I never got much beyond Bethlehem, Pennsylvania, until I moved here. But I've always wanted to see California. I understand it's quite beautiful."

"Yes, it is."

"How did you end up in D.C.?"

"Work. I teach law at American University."

"I'm impressed."

"What about you? Tell me about Liz Callow."

"What do you want to know?"

"Everything!" she says, leaning forward, eyebrows arched to her hairline. "Are you living with anyone?"

"Yes and no."

"Trying to be mysterious? You've got my attention."

"I have my own apartment in Georgetown, but I don't get there much these days. I'm taking care of a friend."

"A friend? This sounds suspicious."

"No, really. I'm taking care of my best friend. She has a serious heart condition."

"Oh, sorry to hear that. I shouldn't have joked."

The screen door opens and a tall woman with glasses and shoulder-length amber hair comes in. She stands behind Kathryn, hands on Kathryn's shoulders.

"Liz, this is JoAnne, my housemate and good friend. JoAnne, Liz Callow."

JoAnne offers her hand. "Nice to meet you." I squint as I feel her fingers wrap around mine with a pressure that makes me want to faint.

"Sorry," JoAnne says, sitting down next to me. "Sometimes I don't know my own strength."

"JoAnne is our resident body builder, weight lifter and health food nut," Kathryn says, rolling her eyes.

A square jaw and deep set eyes reveal a toughness about JoAnne that is somehow gentle, endearing. Despite her sweatshirt, I observe a ripple of muscles running across her shoulders and down each arm.

"So, you're the woman Kate's been talking about," she says, brushing her hair back with her right hand.

"I must have quite a reputation by now."

"Quite a good reputation."

"It'll wear off once you get to know me."

"Gosh, now wherever did Kate find a modest woman? I've been trying to find one for years."

Kate laughs. "JoAnne's used to me, and modest I'm not."

"So what do you do to amuse yourself besides weight-lifting?" I ask JoAnne, trying to change the subject.

"Well, one of my other hobbies you're about to witness. The rest of the time I work as a crane operator for Capitol Construction."

"That must be interesting."

"Would you believe, boring?"

We talk a few minutes longer until the rest of the guests begin to mill around outside, sitting at tables and standing along the walls.

JoAnne gets up, patting me on the back. The force nearly sends me to the floor. "I like you. You're cute," she says, disappearing into the house.

A few minutes later, JoAnne returns with a guitar and a small stool which she sets up in the front of the room. Kathryn leans across the table, patting my arm to get my attention.

"JoAnne plays in some clubs in the city. She's very good."

The music is excellent, a variety of folk and contemporary songs everyone seems to know. People sing and clap, clearly enjoying themselves. As JoAnne continues with her performance, I find myself staring at Kathryn. Her attractiveness is seductive — the strong lines of her face accentuated by the shadows. From a distance I feel the energy surrounding her, a mystique that keeps me away as much as it draws me nearer.

Kathryn turns and catches me staring. She takes my hand, squeezing it gently. Leaning, close enough so no one else can hear, she whispers, "I'm glad you're here tonight."

I glance at my watch. It's after two a.m. I'm

sitting on Chris's front porch sipping a beer, trying to make sense of my thoughts. An hour ago I'd said my good-byes and thank-you's to Kathryn and JoAnne. Instead of driving to my apartment after the party, I'd decided to come back to the farm. I want to talk to Chris, to smooth things out, to apologize for the misunderstanding earlier that evening. I've been struggling for the right words, but the beer and the late hour make things hazy. A fog has settled over my brain, hiding answers I want desperately to find.

I let myself into the house. In the kitchen, the dog greets me.

"Hi, girl. Now you be quiet. Sit here with me. We don't want to wake your mother."

After getting a beer from the refrigerator, I sit in the chair next to the side porch. I think about the evening's events — the fight with Chris, meeting Kathryn. And I wonder how I'll ever get my equilibrium back.

"Buddie, what are you doing here?"

Chris is standing in the kitchen doorway, clutching a blue terry-cloth robe around her. Trying to adjust my vision, I get up. But I'm dizzy so I sit back down. Reaching for my beer I tell her, "Watch out, I'm drunk."

"I can see that. Are you all right?"

I look at her through an emotional haze. "I just spent the entire evening in the company of about thirty women. I can't be that bad off, can I?"

"Seems you had a better time than expected."

"It was interesting."

"So, who were all these women?" Chris asks, sitting down across from me.

"Oh, yes," I say, pointing at her defiantly. "By all means, take a safe seat."

"Buddie, we can't talk when you're like this."

"We couldn't talk before either."

Chris gets up and walks over to me, placing her arms around my neck. "I know I hurt you, Buddie, and I'm really sorry. In fact, that was the whole problem — I was feeling sorry for myself." She sits back down in the chair next to me, running her hands across the table's smooth surface. "And jealous."

"Jealous? Of what, for God's sake?"

She shrugs. "Of you. Getting on with your life."

"Chris, you're a big part of my life. Nothing's ever going to change that."

"You'll keep helping me through the bad moments, won't you, Buddie? Even if I do act like a shithead."

"Of course. I'm sorry, too. I was out of line earlier."

"No, you weren't. You were just trying to tell me something. I wasn't listening."

"Are you listening now?"

"Yes."

"I love you."

"I know. I love you, too."

"Want a beer?"

"No," she replies laughing. "And you don't either. It's time for bed. And if you don't come quietly, it'll be the couch for you, the same one I reserve for my worst enemies."

"Oh no, not that."

Chris takes the beer out of my hand and leads me upstairs. My last thoughts are of her — putting covers over me, turning out the light and kissing me on the forehead just above my right eye.

Chris leaves a couple of weeks before Thanksgiving to spend the holidays with her sister in Colorado. Until she returns at the end of the year, I take care of the farm. Maggie is my constant companion. Lonely for Chris, she settles for me as a temporary replacement.

"C'mon, girl. Time to feed the horses."

The horses — Shin, Bridget and Coal — belong to the landlord who owns the farmhouse Chris rents. Mr. Covington, a retired engineer, is also away vacationing in Florida. With patient instruction from Chris, I've learned how to care for the horses.

The creaking doors of the barn swing wide into the paddock area as Maggie and I enter to a musty smell of corn, oats and hay. I walk the wide floor boards along the middle aisle, stopping at the last stall on the right to greet Bridget, the six-month-old filly who acknowledges me enthusiastically with the toss of her gray head. I pat her cotton-soft coat, her dark chestnut eyes wide with the anticipation of dinner.

Once the feedings are completed, I spread some new hay. Light filters through fissures in the large structure, patterning bright lines across the floor below me. Dust flies and dances along each beam of light, resident barn swallows diving and chattering along the rafters above. I finish with the hay, stacking the newly delivered bundles against the back wall. As I turn to leave, I notice a shadow in the doorway. The shadow moves forward until several stripes of light from the window to my left fall across the face now directly in front of me.

"Am I early?"

"Hi, Kate. Early? I don't know. What time is it?"

"It's almost four-thirty. Isn't that when you said to come over?"

"That's right. Sorry, I got behind on my chores today. Lost track of time."

"So I see. Can I help?"

"I'm finished now."

"Looks like you've been working hard. You're sweating." Kate steps toward me. "And you've got hay in your hair." She brushes her hand through my hair, the light of the nearby window reflecting in her earthen eyes. "I guess this is what life on the farm's really like, huh?"

"Yes, and I'm not sure I'm up to it. C'mon inside. Dinner will take a while to make. I'm planning lasagna, if that's okay."

"My favorite. Hey, Maggie!"

Maggie greets Kate with her usual enthusiasm, jumping up and licking Kate's face, her tail keeping three-quarter time. They've become fast friends.

"Thanks for the kiss, Maggie. Guess I should be happy to have a female kiss me, even if it's the dog." Kate looks at me and laughs. She puts her arm around my shoulder as we walk to the house. "Did you miss me?"

Kate grins after the question. She seems so certain of my answer, I temper it with resistance. "I thought about you a few times."

This response brings genuine laughter. "Only a few times? I think I'm disappointed."

"Kate, we talk on the phone every day. And this is the third time we've had dinner this week."

"Yes, but you crave my company. And I, yours."

"Care for a beer?" I offer, changing the subject.

"Love one, thanks."

Kate follows me around the kitchen, sipping her beer and looking over my shoulder. Her proximity is unnerving. "Do you like to cook? We could talk for a while, then go out to eat." She's leaning on the counter, looking at me sideways, eyes squinting in the afternoon light.

"I don't mind cooking. It relaxes me."

She smiles approvingly. "Good. I hate to cook. I get bored. There's one exception, though. After a night of unbelievable love-making, I like cooking a big breakfast. Providing it's on the weekend, of course — and we don't have to go to work."

"Of course."

"But, if you need help with anything right now, I'd be more than willing."

"Why don't you turn some music on? I'm going to put the lasagna in the oven and then take a shower. Do you mind?"

"Not at all. If you need help getting the hay off, perhaps I can assist." Kate is smiling again as she gets up and goes into the living room. "Don't mind my sense of humor," she yells from the next room. "Or my sense of adventure."

The steaming water is an anesthesia. I stand under it for a long time trying to relax. Wondering what will happen with Kate. Clearly, after all the time we've spent together in the past weeks, the shared chemistry between us is growing. Stepping out of the shower, I reach for a towel on the stool next to the sink. But someone's hand is already on it. I feel the towel brush across my back and over my shoulders. Just behind me, I hear the words as they are softly spoken. "Turn around and look at me."

I turn and look into Kate's eyes, the one place I should never have looked to find escape, but where I might look to find steadiness, strength. I square my jaw to the fluttering sensations in my stomach, the water dripping from my hair into my eyes.

"Are you as scared as I am?" I ask her, beginning to shiver.

Kate takes me into her arms. "No, but I'll pretend."

We fall onto the bed. Kate's still dressed. Her hands are on my breasts, lips kissing my neck. Slowly, I unbutton her blouse, run my tongue across her bra — feel the hard nipples underneath. Kate looks down and smiles, removing the rest of her clothes.

The room is bronze with the fading vestige of the afternoon. Across the sunlit window, Kate's shadow moves. Her eyes are the color of the fields I know from memory — the same color of the sunset now folding into the valley. I hold her forearms as she kisses me, the muscles inside of them twitching against my fingertips, her breath warm on my face. For the past six months I knew I was alive because I had felt the pain of each passing day. But now, finally, pleasure overtakes pain. And I find myself alive, strangely alive in this woman's arms.

"I wanted to make love to you the first moment I saw you," Kate says, the words whispered softly between a kiss.

"Why, Kate? Why me?"

"Because you wanted me, too."

As Kate's body moves gently against mine, I feel a thousand sensations not unknown, simply forgotten. Holding me around the waist, Kate moves her tongue along my right breast, setting my nerves pleasantly on edge. Responding to the sensation, I pull her hand to my thigh. She smiles again, eyes changing hue. Slowly, moving inside of me, Kate's touch is strong, but tender in its motion. I run my fingers through Kate's hair, turning her face toward me as she loves me. There is a seriousness in her gaze now, an eagerness to please. She need not have worried. My head drops onto the pillow as Kate moves deeper inside.

In the back of my mind, beyond the moment, I feel guilt and betrayal to Chris who's not here instead. But Chris and I have never been lovers. Quickly, I shut my mind to that door, compelled to open another. It's the base side of me I hate, streaming forth from the emptiness of recent years, moving me finally to accept the passion of these moments.

Through the trees, just beyond the railroad tracks, the Lehigh River runs cold, splitting Bethlehem, Pennsylvania, in two. The Hill-to-Hill Bridge, connecting the chasm, is now decorated with the traditional pine trees and advent candles which make Bethlehem "Christmas City, U.S.A."

I stand on the tree-lined bank behind my parent's home, the biting cold of winter moving through me. The trees creak against the wind, branches clicking and snapping in the breeze. There will be snow soon.

"Hey, dinner's ready."

My youngest brother, Roger, comes out and stands on the bank beside me, his broad shoulders at least two inches above my own. His short, military-style haircut reveals a slightly receding hairline.

"Everybody's here now. Tom, Anne and the kids arrived about ten minutes ago."

Roger opens the sliding porch door, letting me in ahead of him. The living room is crowded with people. My two older brothers, Tom and Steve, and their wives, Anne and Lois, along with my five nephews, seem to occupy every inch of space.

"What does everyone want to drink?" my mother calls from the kitchen.

I step over one of my nephews, who's busy grinding PlayDoh into the rug in front of me, and proceed to the kitchen where I find my mother in her usual Christmas day frenzy.

"Would you like some help?" I offer, taking tumblers from the cupboard.

"No, I'm fine. Lois has been helping me."

"What can I do?"

"Find a seat at the table."

Exasperated, I sit down next to Roger who puts his arm around my shoulder.

"How you been, Sis?"

"Hanging in there. And you?"

"Busy studying. How's Chris?"

"Tired. Weak. She's been in Colorado staying with her sister's family since before Thanksgiving."

"How long will she be gone?"

"Until New Year's. There's a doctor at the Denver Medical Center that Chris's sister wants her to see. He's been working with some experimental drugs for heart patients. Chris may be a candidate for the program."

"That sounds promising."

"I hope so."

The conversation is interrupted by the arrival of everyone at the table, which is now covered from end to end with steaming platters of food. My stepfather sits at the head of the table, my mother at the opposite end. As is tradition, my stepfather says a brief prayer — its finish signaling the onset of madness. Hands reach from everywhere, children cry, the dog watches from a nearby corner and food ends up on the floor. I wait until the furor subsides, then help myself to what's left.

Without knowing why, I find myself watching my mother. In between bites of food, her eyes are on my brothers. She listens to their every word, eyes darting from one to the other as they discuss topics from sports to politics. Her adoration is hard to miss. I think it's an unconscious fixation arising from some sense of matriarchal duty. It's also an affront I've endured since childhood. Despite the constant struggle for her attention — top grades in school, college scholarships, recognition in my field of work — my mother remained focused on her son's lives. I was the woodwork, the picture on the wall, the shadow in the hallway. When my mother discovered I was a

lesbian, it was a true culmination of all the years —
her open disinterest clearly expressed. I became a
recurrent irritant, like stomach gas after a bad meal.

It was a Sunday in October, over two years ago.

"Buddie, your father and I want to talk to you,"
my mother said, interrupting a conversation with
Roger.

"What's up?"

"Roger, can we talk to Buddie alone?" my mother
asked, turning away from me.

"He can stay," I said, not wanting to be
abandoned. I was already feeling the hostility — a
clear sense of impending doom.

"I'd rather not embarrass you," my mother
replied, a look of displeasure on her face.

"What's this about?"

My stepfather emerged meekly from the shadows
of the kitchen, hands shoved into his pockets. "Isn't
there a better time to discuss this?"

"Hey, I'm getting a little worried now," my
brother said, getting up. "What's going on here?"

My mother sighed with exasperation. "Why don't
you ask your sister?"

The vultures continued to hover, waiting for the
opportune time to strike. "Wait a minute," I said
angrily. "You started this. Please tell me what's on
your mind, so we can get on with life."

My mother wrung her hands, looking as though
the world were about to end any minute. "A friend
of mine came to me last week. She said she saw you
go into one of those bars last Saturday night."

"One of those bars?"

"You know what I mean."

"No, I don't," I replied innocently. I did, of course, but I wanted to force my mother to explain.

"One of those bars . . . for homosexuals."

My brother looked at me, his eyes helplessly searching my own.

"Well, it's true. I did. Not that it's anybody's business."

"It's my business," my mother said quickly. "What were you doing there?"

"Having a beer."

"Why in one of those places?"

"Because, I'm a lesbian, Mother. Makes sense, doesn't it?"

My stepfather sat down across from me and stared blankly at his knees. Standing motionless, my mother couldn't seem to do anything. Finally, after an eternity of silence, she declared, "Nonsense. You're not a lesbian. Why would you even say such a thing?"

"Because it's true."

"Buddie has her own life to lead," my brother added in my defense. "What does it matter, so long as she's happy?"

"You be quiet," my mother snapped. "This does not concern you."

"It certainly does. I've known about Buddie for a long time, Mom. It doesn't make one bit of difference to me, and it shouldn't to you."

"You don't know what you're saying, young man. Your sister is throwing her life away!"

I got up from the dining room table, brushing past my mother and getting my coat from the closet.

It was not my intention to continue with a futile discussion. As I opened the door, I turned to smile at my brother, silently thanking him for the feelings of victory only he had given. Once outside, I was aware of a grim finality at my heels. But there was relief, too, and a sense of control over my life I'd never experienced.

CHAPTER THREE

From the living room window I watch the snow falling, the road covered in a blanket of white three days before New Year's Eve. It's an early snow fall for Virginia, the first one of the season. Nestling in the branches of the pines, the snow creates a dream-world effect, an impressionist's painting that numbs the senses. I put my coat and boots on, grab the ax out of the utility closet, and head outside to get more wood for the fire.

The snow is wet and heavy, about two inches deep and still falling at a good pace. The forecast has called for at least three inches and the pearl-gray sky above promises its del͏-ꞁery.

On the far side ot ᴜhe barn, the wood pile looms endlessly before me. I select some larger logs for later that evening, then begin to chop the others into kindling. Halfway into the last log, I suddenly feel a stinging pressure along the right side of my face. A lump of coldness slides down my jaw, stopping at the base of my neck. Removing a glove, I feel for the damage. Then I hear the laughter behind me. I turn to find Chris bending down, making several more snowballs in preparation for what looks like an all-out battle.

"Hey — no fair!" I yell, moving quickly from the front of the wood pile to the back. "You weren't supposed to be home until tomorrow."

"Surprise!" Another snowball accompanies the remark.

I begin to make my own supply of ammunition, firing a couple of quick shots from my makeshift fort. When they miss their mark, I decide an offensive move is in order. I fill my pockets with as many snowballs as I can and, with a war cry, charge my assailant at full speed. The surprise strategy works — several hits striking the enemy in the chest and legs. When I'm within a few feet of her, I let my final snowball fly. She ducks expertly, the snowball landing on the house behind her. Before I can fully adjust to the situation, a land mine of snow hits me in the face.

"Shit," I say ungraciously. Grabbing a handful of snow and breaking into a run, I chase Chris who is too slow to respond. I tackle her at the waist. As she hits the ground, I hear her laugh.

"You cheat, Buddie."

"Hey, this is hand-to-hand combat," I reply, stuffing a large wad of snow down the back of her coat.

"Awww, no! Buddie, I quit!"

Her complaints are a ruse. She grabs some of the cold stuff and tries to rub it in my face. I pin both of her arms down, the two of us laughing uncontrollably.

"Uncle, Buddie, uncle. I give up." Her face is red from the cold. She is breathing hard. For a moment, I'm frightened.

"Very well, then. I'll release the prisoner." I let go of her arms and lean backward, still sitting on her legs. "Guess we know who won."

"Oh, sure. Take advantage of a sick, helpless person."

"You look fine to me." I mean it. She does look well — eyes bright, good skin color. Breathing back to normal. I lean over, resting my hands above her waist. Chris smiles at me, eyes reflecting the day's white sky. I brush some of the snow from her forehead. "As a matter of fact, you look great."

She sits up, her legs still underneath me. "I was accepted into the drug program, Buddie. I started taking the drug four weeks ago. I feel so much better, stronger. I feel terrific!" Chris puts her arms around my shoulders. Pulling me toward the ground, she hugs me and laughs. "Thanks for being here when I got home."

"That's such good news, Chris. Thank God for modern science."

Chris puts her hands to my face. "There are no guarantees, Buddie. The drug is new. No track record."

"But you feel better. You're stronger. That's what counts."

She kisses the tip of my nose. "You're glad to have me back, aren't you?"

"Yes, I am."

The fireplace crackles, embers glowing red. I prop my feet on the hearth, beer in hand. "This is the life. A fire, a beer and a best friend for company." I lean back in the rocking chair. "What's more, I'm on vacation until the middle of next week."

"You always amaze me, Buddie," Chris replies. "Most people take their vacation in the summer. You wait for January and a blizzard. How was Christmas?"

An ember flies out of the fire and I smash it with the poker. "My mother and I avoided each other. My stepfather and I exchanged only the required pleasantries. I had fun with the kids, though."

"Have you heard anything more from your friend, Kathryn?"

Nervously, I poke at the fire. I knew the subject would come up eventually. Silently, I curse the moment. "Yes, I have. We've spent quite a bit of time together since you left."

"Really? How is she?"

"Good, good. Thought I might bring her here New

Year's Eve. She wants to meet you." I look at Chris. She's staring at the fire, her face expressionless.

"Great. I asked people from the studio over, and some other friends. It'll be a good opportunity to meet her, and I think I should."

"What do you mean?"

"Kathryn's an important person in your life. For that reason alone I want to meet her."

Chris turns and looks at me. The lovely structure of her face has returned, no longer puffy and distorted from steroids. "I'm happy for you, Buddie. I'm glad you met someone."

"I'm not sure what'll happen. She's a strong person, an independent person. Hard to get to know."

"Are you in love with her?"

I struggle with the question, putting my head in my hands, trying to move past sudden confusion.

"I'm sorry, Buddie," Chris says, interrupting my thoughts. "That was a personal question I had no right to ask. It's none of my business."

Suddenly, I get up, no longer sure of anything. "I want to have another snowball fight, Chris. In fact, I want to have a thousand more snowball fights. I want to dive into the snow until I'm blue in the face. C'mon," I say, moving toward the front door. "Let's kill each other with snow."

"Buddie, are you crazy? It's after midnight."

"No crazier than I was this afternoon."

Chris gets up from the floor and comes over to me. "Very well, then. But you'll be sorry."

Opening the door, I grab her by the arm. "Somehow, I doubt that very much."

* * * * *

Outside Gallagher's Pub on Connecticut Avenue, I pace up and down the sidewalk. It's raining but I hardly notice. Kate is twenty minutes late. As I retrace my steps for the hundredth time, I wonder where she is. Finally, I decide to go inside without her. Taking a seat at the crowded bar, I order a beer and pass time by watching television. Not able to hear anything, I try to lip-read. After ten minutes of this nonsense, I start watching people instead.

My study of bar life is interrupted by a hand on my shoulder. I swivel to the right, feeling the touch of cold fingers across my neck. Kate's standing next to me, grinning and leaning over the chair, her elbow resting on the bar. Her presence as commanding as ever.

"Can I buy the lady another drink?" she asks, raising her eyebrows. "Unless, of course, she's waiting for someone else."

"Yes, you can. And no — she's not waiting for anyone else." I take Kate's cold hand from my neck and rub it between my hands. "Kate, where are your gloves?"

"I can never hang onto a pair for very long."

I remove my coat from the seat next to me. Kate sits and calls for the bartender. She is dressed in kelly green pants and a gray hooded sweatshirt damp with the cool droplets of a December rain. Her skin tone is light like pinewood, her cheek bones high and defined. Absentmindedly, she tosses hair from her forehead which reveals three barely perceptible furrows, each about two inches long. They are worry lines that disturb an otherwise flawless face — a hardness that only adds to her attractiveness.

Kate hands me my beer, holding her glass against my own. "Here's to the coming New Year. Cheers."

"Cheers, Kate."

"Am I still expected at the farm tomorrow night?"

"Yes, Chris wants us to help her ring in the New Year."

"I think we can manage that." She hops down from the bar stool. "Let's get a table. I'm starved."

As I listen to Kate talk over the hum of the small restaurant's activities, a kind of depersonalization overcomes me. I feel as though I'm seeing through someone else's eyes. This can't be my life, I think. This woman can't be my lover. Should she be my lover? Confusion reigns.

Kate stops talking. During the brief pause, I try to find myself again. "Did you talk to your family Christmas Day?"

"I talked to my mother."

"It's too bad you couldn't get home for the holidays. I know how much you miss San Francisco."

"It gave me more time to spend with you. Besides, I miss the city, but not always the turmoil I seem to have left behind."

"Turmoil."

"I don't get along very well with my father."

"What about your mother? I'm an expert on that subject."

"My mother's great."

"Do you have any brothers or sisters?"

The candlelight flickers in Kate's eyes as she

surveys the edge of the ceiling just above my head. "No, there's just me."

"Lucky you. I grew up with three brothers. Want one?" I ask jokingly.

Kate's face suddenly goes blank. Then she empties her glass. "I want another beer."

Throughout a somewhat stilted conversation, I learn several more facts about Kate's past. Although we had talked a lot over the past weeks, she seemed reticent to discuss her family. Tonight, she provides a few more details. Her father is an investment banker, her mother active in social and charitable causes. Her parents own a beautifully restored Victorian home in San Francisco and a vacation home about twenty miles outside the city. She talks about her parents in a factual manner, about herself more openly.

"When I was fourteen I started having dreams that I could fly," she says with an amused grin. "Then I fell madly in love with my ninth grade history teacher. Her name was Carol Michaels. She was exciting, intelligent. At first, I couldn't quite place myself in the scheme of things, but it didn't take me long to figure it out." Kate smiles, suddenly changing gears. "Want to go dancing tonight?"

"Dancing? Where?"

"Do you have your car?"

"Yes. I was too lazy to walk to the metro."

"I know a great place. Let's go."

Tracks, a warehouse-district club, is crowded with both men and women on this Saturday night. With one of the largest dance floors in the D.C. area, the club draws large crowds and stays open until six a.m. A cloud of smoke hangs in the air as we push our way to the bar. Miraculously, we find one available seat in the crush of people.

"You sit down," Kate offers. "If I get tired, I'll sit on your lap."

Kate orders two beers. I sit down, turning toward the activity on the dance floor. I watch the moving shadows in front of me, punctuated by flashing colored lights bouncing from one side of the room to the other. People are dancing in groups, in couples — some by themselves. Taken by the music, their bodies move in a wave of activity bound by nothing, not even the music itself.

Kate hands me my beer. Half-sitting, she rests against my thigh for support. I wrap my arms around Kate's waist, pulling her closer. I tell myself she's by far the loveliest woman in the room. Leaning over, I kiss her just below the temple, soft hair brushing against my forehead. She looks up at me and smiles.

"Later, you can give me a proper kiss."

"I'm sure I won't mind," I reply, running my fingers along the base of her neck.

"See those two women over there?" Kate nods toward the closest edge of the dance floor. The two women are facing each other, arms around each other's waist. "They're in here every weekend," she says, continuing her train of thought. "Can't keep their hands off each other. See what I mean?"

I watch the two women kissing, oblivious to the crowd and the noise.

"Must be love," Kate comments, brushing the hair from her forehead. "Must be nice to feel that way."

I look at Kate. Suddenly, I wonder about our

relationship. I wonder if love has anything to do with it.

"Have you ever been in love?" I ask her.

"Yes. But that was a long time ago."

"What about us?"

Kate turns, putting her arms around my neck. "We just met, Liz. It's not time to start thinking about those things. Everything will get complicated. We'll stop having fun."

"Kate, we've been dating for over three months."

"That long? Well, we better plan our engagement party, then," she says, clearly amused.

Kate smiles, straightening my shirt collar and running her fingers along the tops of my ears. Taking a sip from my beer, I try to wash away the lump in my throat. I force a smile to my lips as Kate kisses me on the forehead, the warmth of her skin pressing against an inner numbness.

"Want to dance?" she asks.

Annoyed, I slide off the bar stool. "You must come in here a lot. You seem to know the regulars."

"I come here when I don't have anything better to do," she responds nonchalantly.

"What does that mean?"

"It means I get bored like everyone else."

Not waiting for a reply, she takes my hand and leads me onto the dance floor. The air's warm, almost muggy, as we squeeze into a corner on the far side of the room. She puts her arms around me, her skin a soft shade of blue from the lights above, eyes glassy from the late hour. She pulls me closer and I rest my head on her shoulder, her hands clasped tightly behind my back.

"I remember when I first saw you," she says suddenly, talking quietly.

I pull back, looking at her. Which Kate is this, I wonder?

"I'm not a hard person, Liz. But I've learned to protect myself. It's known as survival." Again she pulls me close, her cheek against mine. "I remember seeing you a little ways ahead of me, fumbling with your recording equipment. You made me smile. Not many people I meet for the first time are able to do that." Kate plays with my shirt collar again, smoothing it out. "Then when you asked your question, you seemed so shy for a reporter. I thought it was sweet. I wanted to meet you again, to know more about you."

"Are you disappointed?"

"No."

We continue dancing into the next song. I concentrate on our movements, the rhythm of the music, the warmth of Kate's body against mine. And I think about the hard shell of her that had briefly cracked — letting me in for a fragmentary glimpse of the feelings whirling inside of her. There's time, I assure myself. There's so much time.

The music ends and we leave the floor. Back at the bar, Kate finds a group of friends. Sitting off to the side, I watch the Kate I'm only beginning to know dazzle them with her carefree spirit. It's a spirit that will be hard to hold.

Twenty minutes pass before I feel a tug at my sleeve. When I turn around, Kate grabs my wrist.

"Come and stay at my house tonight. JoAnne's away. It'll give us some time together."

"Fine." I reach for our coats, wondering where the word I had just spoken came from.

The streets are empty of traffic at this late hour. Kate leans her head against my shoulder, her hands wrapped around my arm. Mentally, I try to pull away from her. It's a half-hearted effort to protect myself from the obvious limits Kate's placed on the relationship. Kate turns in her seat, her warm breath moving across the nape of my neck. Instantly, I find myself drawn back to her. I turn to kiss her forehead, the softness of her skin the only thing I can think of at this moment. It's too late to stop myself, I decide, pulling the car alongside the curb in front of the house. I've already allowed Kate into my life . . . for as long as that time is meant to be.

The bedroom is dark, sheets cold when I move between them. I lie there with my eyes open, trying to adjust to the darkness. The radiator across the room bubbles and hisses. Pulling the covers over my shoulders, I wish for some of its warmth. A shadow jumps up on the bed next to me, moving in my direction. Eventually, I discover myself lying face-to-face with a cat, now resting comfortably on my chest. It extends its paw, softly rubbing the side of my face as if to say hello.

"Well, aren't you friendly?" I scratch its head and the petting elicits a loud purring, its soft neck vibrating with pleasure.

"I see you've met Martha," Kate says as she climbs into bed next to me.

"Yes, she's beautiful. Is she yours?"

"Brought her with me from New York. One of the many strays I took care of. Martha was special. I couldn't bear to leave her behind."

"I'm glad you didn't."

"You like cats?"

"I love animals."

"Always wanted a cat when I was a kid, but my father wouldn't allow it. He hated animals. The first thing I did when I moved out was get a cat. It really pissed him off."

"Why did he care? You didn't live at home anymore."

Propped up on her elbow, Kate rests her chin in the palm of her hand. "Because that's the way my father is. Everything is black and white, cut and dried. He likes to control people; it makes him feel powerful."

"You said you didn't get along with him. Do you talk to him much?"

"Not if I can help it." Kate reaches for my hand as the cat saunters off into the shadows. "I want to hold you now."

I move toward her, pushing away the covers that separate us, the grayness of her face warm against my own. Putting my arms around her I say, "I love you, Kate." Immediately, I chastise myself for having said the words. I never seem to know where to begin, or when to quit.

Kate places her hands on either side of my face, kissing me lightly on my forehead, mouth, neck. As she aligns her body with my own, I feel our skin run together like warm droplets of rain against a sun-filled window. It's a meshing of sensations I can't turn away from.

I run my hands across Kate's breasts, over her stomach and down her thighs. I feel her softness, her trembling excitement, her wetness for me. Kate's hands are on either side of my head, her thighs pressed against my shoulders. As I slowly bring her to a climax, her exhaled breaths quicken, building to a soft cry. Then the rigidness of her body falls gently into the sheets, my head lying on her stomach, her legs crossed around my back.

Later, there is silence in the darkness as Kate's hands massage my shoulders. These are the after-movements of love that need no words. I curl up against her and close my eyes. Listening to her heart beat, I search its sound for tenderness. But I hear only the strength of it, the sureness of each beat, a continuous tone fading inside my head.

The sound of voices wakes me, the bedroom a muffled cocoon distorting my ability to hear. I turn on the light. Three a.m. I glance at the empty bed as a gurgle of voices drifts in from the living room. A loud noise brings me to an upright position. There's a slamming, knocking sound followed by a loud shout. Getting out of bed, I quickly put my clothes on and move toward the doorway. When I open the door the voices stop. Entering the hallway to the living room, I see Kate standing a few feet away from another woman I don't recognize.

"Kate, is something wrong?" I ask, shuffling into the living room, squinting to soften the bright lights.

"Who the hell's that?" the unidentified woman asks in a tone that is hardly complimentary.

"Liz, this is Cory. A friend from New York. She decided to drop by unexpectedly in the middle of the night."

Abruptly, the woman turns to me, and with a rather distasteful sneer says, "Oh. You must be the next victim."

"Cory, that's enough," Kate replies, hands clenched at her hips.

"Ladies, is there going to be a fight? Because if there is, I don't think I want to be involved."

"Look, you," Cory shouts. "If you know what's good for you, you'll want to hear the interesting tale I'm about to tell. Too bad Kate's reputation didn't precede her all the way to D.C."

"All right, Cory. That's enough. You're going to have to leave." Kate points toward the door.

"Not yet, bitch! I came all this way to say a few things, and I couldn't care less if your new girlfriend happens to be here."

"Calm down, Cory."

"Calm down! Please! I've got a lot to be angry about, don't you think? I've written, called — but you've ignored me, Kate."

"Our relationship's over, Cory. It's been over for eight months. Why put us through this?"

"I drove back and forth from New York to Washington every weekend for months. I was looking for a job here. Then all of a sudden it's over? I have a right to know why, Kate."

I want desperately to leave the room, but my feet are stuck to the floor, mind slammed shut on the hardness in Kate's voice.

"I'm not about to dredge up every last deficiency I found in our relationship, Cory. I felt it was better to let things end as they were."

"And how was that, Kate?"

"Completely unsatisfying for me, to be quite honest."

"You cheated on me the entire time, didn't you, Kate?"

"I'm not going to dignify that with an answer."

Cory collapses onto the sofa, face buried in her hands. Without anyone noticing, I turn and go back into the bedroom. Welcoming the darkness, I ignore the hollow sounds still coming from the living room. It's too soon to think.

A few hours later I wake up with a painful buzzing in my head. I put a hand to each temple, softly rubbing the area where the pain has concentrated itself. But it's the noise that bothers me more than the pain — a nagging buzz as though a fly has taken up residence inside my head. I try to relax it away, but it stays — an aggravating beginning to the last day of the year.

Suddenly, Kate's in the doorway, hair wet from a morning shower. She smiles boldly, leaning against the door jamb, arms crossed in front of her.

"Hey, beautiful. Happy almost New Year."

"Happy New Year," I mumble over the buzzing in

my head. "I had a very strange dream last night, Kate."

"I don't think it was a dream."

"Too bad. I was hoping I imagined the whole thing."

"Sorry," she says, entering the room.

Kate sits down on the bed, crossing her legs and leaning a forearm on each thigh. "Hungry?"

"I hope you didn't send that poor woman home to New York in the middle of the night."

She looks at me and smiles. "You must think I'm a real schmuck. Cory just left about ten minutes ago. She fell asleep on the couch."

"Well, the way things were progressing last night, I wasn't sure what was going to happen."

"Let's get something to eat. This time, I'll cook."

"I'm not very hungry."

"Sure you are."

Once in the kitchen, Kate tosses me a small box she's removed from a cabinet. "Hey, open these for me, will you?"

I inspect the package. "Chocolate-covered raisins?"

"Yes, they're a passion of mine. Sometimes, they're all I eat for breakfast."

As I open the box, I add one more tidbit to the list of things I didn't know about Kate, the list that's growing longer by the minute.

I watch Kate as she cooks, wondering what really happened between her and Cory. I'm somehow convinced she's already put the entire incident aside, as though it'd been nothing more than a minor annoyance.

Staring over the rim of my coffee cup, I think

about our own relationship, how Kate and I met, the party at this house. Everything since then had happened so fast. Not used to life in quick doses, I struggle to make sense of why I'm here, of why Kate seems to want me here. I quickly realize that any misunderstandings have been my own fault. If my being here is temporary, then I'm the one who's been dishonest. I've been dishonest with myself. Afraid to face the truth, I never asked Kate what the rules were, or what, if anything, the future might hold. I let things happen as quickly as I wanted them to happen. I wanted Kate to want me — no matter what the cost.

"Kate, what happened with you and Cory?" I ask, interrupting her role as Sunday chef.

She's about to crack an egg, but puts it down, looking at me with incredulous eyes. "That's a personal question, don't you think?"

"Not really."

Kate's angry, her eyes darting from side to side. Her mouth is set, movements rigid — and there's a coldness in her voice that stings. "I thought you might understand. Cory and I grew apart. People change, Liz. I felt suffocated. I can't handle being controlled."

Kate sits in the chair across from me. Her words are soft now, almost inaudible. I have to strain to hear.

"Cory thought she knew me, but she didn't. Maybe that was my fault. There was an emptiness in my life I hadn't resolved. She caught the brunt of it. I won't sit here and say I did all the right things.

But I don't feel I should have to defend myself."
Kate gets up and goes toward the kitchen window.
She hesitates a few moments before finishing her
thoughts. "People think they own you in a
relationship. They expect you to hand your life over
to them on a silver platter. I won't do it that way.
And if that's what you expect of me, then maybe it's
good we're having this conversation now." Kate looks
at me, waiting for a response.

"I only want us to get to know each other, Kate.
I have no intentions of controlling you. Eventually, I
hope we'll grow to need each other, for whatever the
reason."

"Then let's not worry or dwell on the past.
There's no point in it. None at all."

That evening, Kate and I walk hand in hand to
the front porch of the farmhouse. I ring the doorbell
and a few moments later Chris answers.

"Buddie, you didn't have to ring the bell." Chris
takes Kate's hand. "You must be Kate. I'm Chris
Bannister."

Kate puts her arms around Chris's shoulders. "I
feel like I already know you. I think that deserves a
hug, not a handshake."

The living room and kitchen are filled with
people. A few of them I know; the rest are strangers.
They're artists, people familiar with Chris's work,
friends who share a common profession. There are
also a few people I recognize from Chris's studio and

art supply store located at DuPont Circle. Farmers, cashiers and suppliers who work with her on a regular basis.

Chris takes our coats. "What would you guys like to drink?"

"A beer would be fine," Kate replies.

"I'll have the same."

Chris disappears into the kitchen. "Interesting group," Kate comments, stroking her chin. "Mostly a straight crowd from what I can tell."

Chris returns with our beers. "Buddie's told me a lot about you, Kate."

"Am I as stunning as Liz mentioned?" Kate extends her arms outward, imitating a fashion model.

Chris hesitates, then breaks into a smile. "I think she did a good job of describing you."

"Ahhh, but Liz didn't tell me what a knockout you are."

"Jesus, Kate." I feel myself turn pink.

"What beautiful brown eyes you have," Kate says, peering into Chris's face. "Yes, Liz has been holding out on me."

"Buddie, I think you've got a live one here. How do we keep her out of trouble?"

"That's not possible, or probable." I head toward the kitchen. "Think I'll mingle. Maybe I'll find some down-to-earth folk."

From the kitchen I watch Chris and Kate talking and laughing. As usual, Kate does most of the talking, keeping Chris amused. There's an extraordinary charm to Kate's manner, a kind of undeniable magic that overtakes people and puts them at ease. It's a quality hard not to admire.

"Hi, I don't think we've met. Sara Chapman. A friend of Chris's."

A tall, elegant woman with copper-colored hair is standing in front of me. Her face is round and fair — sweet and pleasant.

"Buddie Callow."

"Lovely to meet you, Buddie. Chris has talked about you often. I hear you on the radio."

"How do you know Chris?"

"I own Chapman's Art Gallery on Pennsylvania Avenue. Maybe you've heard of it."

"Of course."

In my mind I quickly run through the various articles I'd seen in the *Washington Post*. Chapman's Gallery is one of the finest galleries in the city. Sara Chapman's a wealthy divorcee who, ironically enough, dumped her husband for a woman about two years ago. An influential gallery owner, she'd established the careers of many fine new artists. A personal showing in the Chapman Gallery means almost certain success for an artist.

Sara Chapman takes a sip of wine, her right arm covered with gold jewelry from wrist to elbow. "You probably know, Buddie, that I'm quite interested in Chris's work. I'm thinking seriously of giving Chris an opportunity for a private showing at my gallery. Maybe sometime this summer."

"Chris must be very excited."

"We've got some details to work on."

"I'm sure she'd welcome the opportunity."

Sara Chapman smiles, absentmindedly smoothing out the green knit dress clinging to her hips. "I'm also president of the Capitol Arts Board. But then, being a reporter, that's old news to you. If things go well at the gallery, I think the board will consider Chris's work for a special exhibit of contemporary women artists from the Washington area. It's an exhibit I've personally been pushing for at the National Museum of Women in the Arts. But I don't think it will happen until early next year."

"I'm sure Chris appreciates your interest, especially after everything she's been through."

"Yes. She, more than anyone, could benefit from some good news."

In the living room, I hear salutations of Happy New Year. From the midst of the noise, Chris comes running into the kitchen.

"C'mon you two. We've got to make a toast. It's almost midnight."

Chris pulls Sara and me into the living room where everyone is busy hugging and singing "Auld Lang Syne."

Kate grabs my arm and turns me toward her. "Hey, what's the big idea, flirting with another woman?" She puts her hands around my waist. "I hope you at least saved me the New Year's kiss."

"Kate, for God's sake, I wasn't flirting. That's Sara Chapman. Chris may get a showing at her gallery."

"Whatever you say."

Kate hugs me and kisses me sweetly. Then she whispers, "We'll save the best for later tonight. I've got a bottle of champagne waiting for us at my house."

Chris taps Kate on the shoulder. "If you two are finished, I'd like to get a picture of the three of us."

"I'll take it for you," Sara offers.

Sara directs us to our places — Chris in the middle, Kate and I on either side of her. "Now, let me see your loveliest smiles. Put your arms around each other. At least pretend you're friends."

Following Sara's instructions, Kate and I put our arms around Chris's shoulders. Kate is laughing and whispers something into Chris's ear.

"Sara, are you going to make us say 'cheese' or something?" Chris asks.

"If I must. Okay, get ready. Say cheese."

The Polaroid camera flashes and whirs, popping out a pale green square. I look over Sara's shoulder, surprised by what I see, by what the camera must have seen. Kate's face displays the same beautiful smile I'd been drawn to the first day we met. Looking at the photograph, I fall hard once again for the confident, intelligent woman I'm struggling to know and understand.

Next to Kate, Chris looks vibrant and well — as healthy as I've seen her in the last six months. There's a renewed spark of life in her eyes, a spark giving back the hope I never wanted her to lose.

I'm on the end, turned slightly to my right, looking toward the two women who have taken loneliness from my life.

Kate looks at the picture, then hands it to Chris. "These are three foxy looking women, no doubt about it."

"I'm going to put this away for safe keeping." Placing the picture inside her desk drawer, Chris returns to the center of the room. "Now, how about that toast," she says, hugging both Kate and me. "We've got a lot to be thankful for. It's going to be a great year."

CHAPTER FOUR

Through the glass separating the news booth and control room, I watch Kevin Tyler select the next hour's music. Listening to the commercial droning on and on inside my headset, I shuffle through the stack of yellow sheets containing the day's news stories. The commercial finally ends. I flip the mike switch on, beginning the broadcast with the lead story.

"This is Liz Callow with a WASH-FM news update. Two men forced their way into a Columbia Heights convenience store late last night, leaving one person dead and one wounded."

I speak the words without hearing them. Mechanically, I continue reading while a thousand other thoughts come in flashes and scattered pieces without beginning or end. It is the last week of March, the days moving quickly past me as I try to assimilate what's constantly changing.

The experimental drug Chris is taking continues to work. She seems to be feeling like her old self again and is looking ahead to a productive summer. But of course I still worry about her anyway.

My relationship with Kate is stationary, a half-in, half-out of my life affair stretching no further than the present. Days with Kate swing like a pendulum in ever-widening arcs above my head. As soon as I begin to zero in on the meaning of our moments together, I lose my grasp and Kate seems more distant than ever.

"I thought maybe tonight we could have a cozy dinner together. Somewhere romantic."

"Liz, I think it'd be a good idea if we did a little socializing for once. I made plans to meet some friends. But if you don't want to come along, that's fine."

"I thought a quiet evening together would be nice. We don't get much time to talk."

"What do you want to talk about?"

"Us. But I guess that wouldn't take more than five minutes, would it?"

"If you're upset about something, Liz, why don't you come right out and say it?"

"I'm not upset. I just think we could be closer."

"We're in bed together. How much closer can we be?"

A phone call I received from Roger several nights ago brings a final thought as I reach the conclusion of the newscast. He's planning a visit to Washington for a few days this weekend. He wants to talk to me about something important. I worry about what that might be, like I worry about everything.

A sensation on my shoulder startles the breath from my lungs.

"Liz, what the hell's going on?"

I look up to find Kevin staring down at me. He's no longer in the control booth, but standing next to me with a pained expression on his face.

"You stopped reading in the middle of a story! I had to put a song on for Christ's sake."

"I'm sorry, Kevin. I don't know what happened."

"Jesus, Liz. I hope Harry didn't hear that. He'll have your ass."

"I'm not feeling well. Guess I should've stayed home today." I get up, disconnect my headset and grab the pile of news stories. "You know, the promotion to news director is great. Hell, the extra money is great. But the hours stink. I may never adjust to getting up at four a.m."

Back in the newsroom, my frustrations get the best of me. Slamming the headphones down on my desk, I curse myself for the lapse in concentration.

"Damnit, what's wrong with me?" I ask myself, sitting at my desk dejectedly.

Pat, our assistant news director, looks up from

her desk on the other side of the room. "Hey, Liz —
you okay? I noticed you sort of stopped talking in the
middle of the last story."

"Not sort of. I did. Damnit!"

"Are you sick?"

"Can you do the last newscast?"

"Sure. You going home?"

"Yes."

"Hey, boss. Good job on that newscast."

It's Doug, the sarcasm in his voice causing an
immediate rise in my blood pressure.

"No wonder you got promoted. They sure do
know talent around here."

He walks past me to his desk. I look at the
glistening letter opener lying a few inches from my
right hand, but decide quickly that lifelong
imprisonment is not for me.

*

I walk into the store, a bell jingling as I enter.
Inside it's quiet. Chris's shop is divided into three
sections — art supplies, a small gallery of prints and
paintings and a framing workshop. A few people are
browsing along the aisles of art supplies. In the back,
a couple picks out a frame for a wedding photograph.

Chris is working in the studio, a room filled with
the perfect light of a sunny afternoon. Her back is
toward me as she paints, the brush moving delicately
over a large canvas in front of her.

For some time, I stand quietly watching her
recreate images from within. Although dwarfed by the
huge size of the canvas, there's no question of Chris's
mastery over its space. Her hands move gracefully in

their art, like a conductor to music. Guiding her inner vision, she channels it into color and light and shadow.

In two months Chris will have a private showing of her work at Chapman's Gallery. After ten years of hard work, the chance for success and recognition is only weeks away.

The sunlight softly outlines Chris's form, obliterating sharp lines and heavy shadows. I move toward her, hands in my pockets for fear I might reach out, as my heart reaches quietly from within.

"I'm still waiting for you to paint a portrait of me. It's something the world should have for posterity. Either that, or my mother for her living room."

Chris turns, sunlight hitting her face, eyes brighter than its light. "Buddie, what a surprise. What brings you to the neighborhood?"

"You, what else? Have time for lunch?"

"What time is it?"

"Almost twelve-thirty. I thought we could walk down to that bagel shop on Connecticut."

Chris steps toward me, brush still in hand. She smiles, its soft edges touching me. "Buddie, I'd love to have lunch with you, but I can't. I'm on a roll here and shouldn't stop."

"I understand." Turning toward the window, I hide my disappointment.

The sound of approaching footsteps ends the discussion.

"Uh, excuse me," an unfamiliar voice interrupts.

I turn toward the voice. A man stands in the

sunlight, his stance slightly crooked. He holds a baseball cap, rolled up like pastry — his hands wringing it. He's tall and muscular, the smoothness of his shoulders visible through a gray and blue flannel shirt.

"Hope I'm not interrupting anything," he says, taking a few steps in our direction.

Chris meets him half way. She stands in between us, her eyes darting back and forth. "Bob, this is Buddie. You remember me talking about Buddie, don't you?"

Bob shoves the hat part way into his pants pocket. "Nice to finally meet you, Buddie."

I'm stunned, arms so heavy I'm sure they'll detach themselves from my body. Bob. The same Bob who abandoned her when she needed him most. The Bob who slithers in and out of her life like a snake in the garden. Bob, Bob, Bob — my mind repeats the name so there can be no mistake. I look at Chris, my mouth empty of words, my mind filled with them. As Bob moves toward me, Chris turns away. I bite my lower lip.

"Buddie, Chris told me what a big help you've been to her. I want to thank you." Bob offers his hand, but my arm is a dead weight, hanging uselessly by my side.

"I've got to go," I say, willing my legs to move toward the door that seems a full football field away. Over the buzzing in my head, I mumble something that sounds like words. "See you later Chris."

"Buddie, I'll phone you tonight."

"You ready for lunch?" I hear Bob ask as I reach

the door. A kind of explosion goes off inside my head, like the kick start of a motorcycle. Somehow I keep stumbling forward, my legs a sorry match for the anger rising within.

My brother walks into the restaurant, his boyish face and jade-colored eyes a welcome sight. Roger takes the seat across from me, then reaches out to touch the side of my face with his hand. "How are you, Sis?"

"Great, now that you're here."

The waitress brings us each a glass of beer and we order dinner. Drumming the table top, my brother sips his beer, leaning back in his chair.

"Do you remember a couple of years ago when I was still in the Army? I converted to Catholicism."

"I remember. The parents split a gut over that one."

He smiles. "There're some new developments." Putting down his glass, Roger reaches for my hand. "I've decided what I want to do after I finish college. I'm going to the seminary in Philadelphia this fall. I want to study for the priesthood."

I look into my brother's eyes; he's serious. I can sense the commitment in his voice. "You've obviously given this a lot of thought."

"It's what I want." His voice conveys excitement. "This is the way I can make a difference, make some kind of meaningful contribution to other people's lives."

"Then I think you should do it. Life's too short to compromise your beliefs."

My brother grins with satisfaction. "Thanks, Buddie. I knew I could count on you for support."

"Isn't that what you've always given me? What we've always given each other?"

The waitress brings our dinner. My brother's suddenly quiet and I think I know why.

"When are you going to tell Mom and Dad?"

"Well," he says, poking at his steak. "I thought one day I'd just show up in my cassock and see what happens."

"Mom will think you died. That you're a ghost."

"Mom will rather I had died."

"I don't think it'll be that bad."

My brother laughs, throwing his head back at the humor of the situation. "I never thought I'd see the day you'd defend Mom."

"I'm not defending her," I say, jabbing his arm with my fork. "She's going to be pissed as hell. But I don't think she'll wish you were dead. Of course, I've been wrong before."

There's a mischievous grin on my brother's face. "I guess it's you and me now, Buddie. We're going to be the black sheep of the family, aren't we?"

"Thank God I've got some company."

"Yes, you can thank God," my brother agrees. "Most definitely."

I'm the one laughing now, head in my hands. "A lesbian and a priest. I almost do feel sorry for Mom."

"Liz, I've been trying to call you all day. Get in here."

Kate stands in the doorway, hair wet and dripping

on my shoes, a piece of peanut butter toast in her hand. She puts her arm around my shoulder and leads me inside, the peanut butter toast dangling just above my breast.

"Want a bite?" she asks turning to face me, extending the toast in my direction.

"No, thanks."

I nod toward the kitchen. "What's going on?"

"JoAnne's having a Friday night bingo party. The kitchen is swarming with her bingo buddies."

Kate finishes her toast, then puts her arms around my waist. "Are you okay?" she asks. "You look like a woman in need. Of me, I hope."

"I'm fine. Just got my brother settled in my apartment for the next few days."

Kate squeezes my hand. "Let's go upstairs. Maybe we can have some privacy up there."

In the grayness of the room, I sit and wait for Kate to blow dry her hair. A few moments after the dryer shuts off, Kate's hand is underneath my chin. She raises my head to look at her. She's still in a robe, her hair curled back from her forehead. She leans down and kisses me lightly on the neck. "Mmmm, you smell good. New perfume?"

"Yes, a present from my brother."

Kate takes off my jacket and folds it neatly, placing it on the chair next to the window. As she unbuttons my shirt, her eyes never leave mine. There is a gentleness in her face tonight, an uncharacteristic softness around the eyes I don't remember seeing before.

"I've been thinking about this all day," Kate says, the rest of my clothes falling to the floor beneath me. I rest my head on Kate's shoulder as she caresses the back of my neck. "You had a bad day, didn't you Liz? Come to bed."

There's moonlight across Kate's back; I watch its illumination as her hands move across my breasts. A tongue runs along my nipple, the warmth turning cold then warm again. With each touch, each kiss, thoughts of the day run away. There's only Kate. Touching me. Loving me. Wanting me.

I grab Kate's shoulders as her hand moves between my thighs, feeling its way inside me. "I can come just watching you," she whispers softly.

A few minutes later, reaching into a nothingness, I flex my toes and close my eyes, riding the interminable stabs of pleasure to the edge, finally dropping into a center of whiteness in the back of my mind. My legs go numb; drops of perspiration run down my jaw-line.

Kate wraps herself around me until her body seems to become my own, her breath cool along my forehead. I touch her face, caress the back of her ear. She kisses me, pulling the covers over us.

"Feel better?" she asks, holding me against her.

"I may never walk again."

"Then I'll carry you to my bed every night."

Sitting up, I lean over the soft shadow beneath me. "I love you, Kate. I need you in my life."

"I know." Kate grabs my arms, pulling me on top of her. "And right now I need your love."

I trace the outline of Kate's face, wanting to remember forever the beauty of it as she lies beneath me. She wraps her legs around me as I kiss her, the contentment in her eyes matching my own.

As I love Kate, there's a stillness in the room, interrupted occasionally by shouts of "Bingo" from the room below. We giggle at the voices and then lie quietly for a while in each other's arms.

Suddenly, there's a knock at the door. Kate's hands tense as I move away from her.

A voice calls in, "Hey, is there sex going on in that room?"

Rubbing her eyes, Kate sits up. "Yes, there is. So please go away."

"Kate, it's JoAnne. Sorry to bother you, but there's someone downstairs to see you."

"Christ! Tell them to go away. Who is it?"

"I don't know her. Maybe someone from the university."

"This is getting to be a habit," I tell Kate as she puts on her robe.

"This is fucking ridiculous. I'm sorry. I won't be long."

Kate opens the door, the light from the hallway bursting into the room. JoAnne pokes her head inside the door and winks. "Hi ya, kid. Havin' fun?" A click, then the room is dark again.

I stretch out across the bed, wondering who Kate's visitor is, remembering the night several months ago when Cory arrived unexpectedly. Thinking my life must carry some kind of curse, I envision my mother standing in front of a roaring fire, a voodoo doll in one hand, a stack of pins in the other. With great satisfaction, she places curse after curse on my love life, willing visitors to Kate's door whenever we're in bed together.

True to her word, Kate returns quickly. She takes

off her robe and holds it out to me. "You'll be needing this."

"Why?"

"It's Chris. She's been looking for you."

"Chris?"

"She wants to talk to you. Guess this makes us even."

I put on the robe and stumble over my shoes. "Shit."

"My sentiments exactly," Kate whispers as I close the door behind me.

Chris is standing near the front door, staring at the living room rug. She looks upset. As I walk into the room she smiles meekly, turning halfway toward the door.

"Sorry to bother you," she says, still avoiding eye contact. "I was worried about you."

"I'm fine."

"I know you must be angry with me and I certainly don't blame you. The way I lied about wanting to work over lunch — that was really crummy."

"You didn't tell me you were seeing Bob again. Why?"

"I knew you'd be upset."

"I just don't want you to get hurt again. You've been through enough hell."

"I'll be careful."

"That's all I care about. You don't have to tell me everything that's going on in your life, Chris. But finding out the way I did today was painful. I felt like a jerk."

"I'm sorry, Buddie. Forgive me?"

"Of course."

Chris turns and opens the door. "I'll call you tomorrow, okay? Maybe we can have dinner."

"I'd like that."

The next day I go out to Chris's place for dinner. We've made our peace with each other and, after a delicious meal of Chicken Divan, we play cards.

"Gin," I say, spreading my cards across the table.

Chris peers at me, a look of perplexity on her face. "Are you cheating?"

"Cheating! How can you say such a thing? I have simply mastered the game of gin."

Chris grabs the cards from the table. "Crap! I hate a smug winner."

"But you love me."

"Can you be nice and get me a soda, please?"

"Yes, of course." But I continue sitting, trying to comprehend the strangeness, the orangeness of the night sky visible through the window directly behind Chris. "God, that's weird. Kind of like a sunset at midnight. Maybe it's a meteor or something." I get up from my chair, mesmerized by the eerie flashes.

"What are you talking about, Buddie?"

"The sky. It's really strange. Come look at it. It's sort of glowing."

"Buddie, no more beer for you."

As I reach the kitchen sink, I look into the side yard. It's glowing like the sky, incredibly orange. It's all around the barn. The barn. My God, the barn's on fire! Flames as high as the pines shoot from the south side of the barn. The horses!

"Chris, the barn's on fire!"

"What? What?" she screams, running to the window. "Oh my God, Buddie. The barn, the horses!"

"Call nine-one-one. I've got to get to the horses."

"Buddie, no! You can't go out there."

"Call nine-one-one. Just do it!" I rush past Chris to the linen closet. Grabbing two large towels, I run back to the sink, soaking them completely in cold water. Before I can comprehend exactly what I'm doing, there's the sound of a slamming door and a rush of cold air.

The air near the barn is hot. Terrified screams from the horses temporarily erase my own fears. Putting one of the wet towels over my head, I open the barn door. Heavy, black smoke billows into the yard. Crouching low, I enter.

To my right, the fire is eating away the south wall. Keeping as far to the left as possible, I arrive at the first stall. Coal is kicking frantically at the boards in front of him, trying to escape. Already gagging on smoke, I loosen the hinge to his stall. As it springs open, horse legs kick at me. Using the extra towel, I throw it over the horse's head, pulling roughly at his mane. Coal moves forward from the stall with me dangling at his side as I try to steer him toward the open door. When we reach the outside, I remove the towel from Coal's face and he's quickly into the field and gone.

Taking several gasps of fresh air, I turn back toward the barn, its outer frame beginning to give off low, creaking sounds.

"Buddie, for God's sake, don't go back in there!" It's Chris, running frantically across the lawn. "Wait for the fire department!"

"If I wait, it'll be too late."

Back inside the shuddering structure, I find the fire is spreading quickly. Again, I lower myself, this time to a crawl. Moving along the left side of the interior, I eventually reach Shin. She's standing quietly as if in shock. Clawing at the hinge, I release her from the stall and place a towel over her head.

"Good girl, Shin."

As we move toward the door, a piece of burning wall falls behind us and Shin panics, kicking me solidly in the right knee. My knee buckles, but instinctively, and out of overwhelming fear, I stagger to my feet and guide the mare to the door. Removing the towel from Shin's eyes, I shove her into the cool night.

The interior of the barn is ghostly, crumbling from the outside in. The black smoke funnels itself through gaping holes and cracks into the night air.

Inside, it's hot, hotter than any stove I've ever touched. My breaths are short and tight, eyes raw and burning. I place a towel over my face, rubbing it into my eyes, trying to breathe through it — gasping for whatever oxygen is left.

Crawling along the floor, my right knee pulsating with pain, I make slow progress toward Bridget's stall, the last one on the right, where the fire is concentrated and out of control.

"Oh, Bridget. Please be alive."

Deadened, hissing sounds and the cracking and crumbling of wood make it difficult to listen for any signs of life from the young filly. Showers of smoldering sparks fall like fireworks around me, and I can no longer see Bridget's enclosure, still a few feet ahead.

"Bridget! Bridget!"

The south wall falters now, falling in from my right. Hot and burning, several boards strike me on the back. I shake them off, lose my nerve and turn toward the open door. My heart pounds against my chest. Then I hear the young horse cry out. I turn and scramble toward her, sparks and ashes burning my hands. Suddenly, I feel a thumping vibration. It's Bridget's body falling to the floor, I tell myself. *Time to get out, Buddie. Time to get out.*

Choking on the ash-filled air, I turn again toward the open door, the night, the coolness. I close my eyes and crawl, concentrating on every painful motion. The floor burns my arms and legs. My right arm aches from shoulder to fingertip, my right knee throbs. My whole body hurts.

Finally, I can feel the lip of the doorway. Pulling myself into the opening, I fall out against the ground, rolling toward the fence. With a jolting bump, I stop — head facing a fence post.

Voices shout. Wetness in the air. Lifting my head, I open my eyes. But I see only the post — its dark wood cracked with age. Then a bright light shines and quickly fades.

I lay my head back down on the cool earth, the shadow-filled blackness inside my head offering a kind of permanence I find comfort in. A gurgling, hissing sound accompanies the blackness, the sound of my own lungs — a heavy, pressing sound that spins me out of consciousness.

CHAPTER FIVE

In a church, surrounded by strangers, she stood next to her brothers, Tom and Steve. Feeling quite a bit older than her ten years, she was about to watch her mother remarry. The organ music started and people filed into the massive room. Finally, her mother walked down the aisle escorted by her grandfather. A pleasant-faced man, a man she did not know, stood at the altar waiting for her mother. She looked around at the pews filled with people and felt very much alone. They were all strangers, and she wondered if she could let them into her life.

While her mother and the pleasant-faced man talked to each other, she thought about her father who had died four years earlier. There were things about him she remembered, faint images that came and went in a blur.

She could almost hear his laughter as he carried her on his shoulders in the backyard. As they circled a plum tree, she clutched his neck tightly, his bouncing step jiggling her up and down. One moment she was brave. She let go of her father's shoulder and reached skyward to touch the leaves of the tree. Grabbing one from its branch, she squeezed it into her hand like some wanted treasure. Then her father twisted her around, holding her in front of him, his blue eyes shining in the sun. He tossed her into the air and caught her, speaking words she couldn't remember. His tanned and handsome face smiled, and she giggled, tickling his nose with the crinkled green leaf. The next moment she was down on the ground, leaning over freshly turned dirt at her father's grave, wondering what had happened to the strong man who had thrown her so effortlessly into the warm summer air. He was gone — a nightmare that had come too soon, and would stay too long.

At the age of thirteen she wore a black armband for the soldiers who had died in the Vietnam War. She saw the marches on Washington from a television screen — the ceremonial coffins draped in black, flowers stuck delicately into the ends of guns. She watched the war every night on the six o'clock news: bombings and defoliation, napalming and a growing list of dead, a list of names so long it made her cry. Until it made her angry. How could this be happening in the world? Her friends worried about getting a date for the junior high school dance. She stayed home and read books like *Johnny Got His Gun* by Dalton Trumbo.

She was a teenager and a rebel; a high school student and a loner; a college senior and an outcast in everyone's mind but her own. And then she came to live on her own and went to work as a junior staff writer at the local newspaper. She wrote obituaries, covered city council meetings, made the morning coffee.

Mostly, she was alone. In the past, there had been crushes on teachers and friends and, as a child, she had heroes, all women — strong and beautiful, intelligent and popular. But until she met Sherri Stamford, she'd always been in the shadows watching and wanting, never knowing why.

Sherri moved into the apartment above her own. She drove a pale blue Pinto with white pin stripes and a rear chrome fender held in place by a single coil of rusted wire. It was, by anyone's account — including Sherri's — a hideous looking car.

One day, she found herself sitting outside on the front stoop, watching the Pinto limp up the street until it angled into the front curb with a jarring bounce. Flat tire. Two long, shapely legs emerged from the car, stomping their way toward the back of the wreck. Sherri wore a skin-tight, black cocktail dress that barely reached the middle of her thighs, its low-cut neckline revealing ample cleavage. After surveying the damage, a well-aimed spiked heel slammed into the back fender. With a loud clank, steel hit macadam.

She worked for an hour helping Sherri change the

tire while those long legs, covered with sheer, silky hose, stood seductively on the edge of her peripheral vision. The sweat and dirt seemed a small price to pay.

To reward her efforts, Sherri invited her upstairs for drinks. As a part-time bartender and waitress, Sherri's special talent was mixology. One Tom Collins and two very dry martinis later, they were both entangled on the sofa. Sherri straddled her lap, thighs open and exposed, bare breasts at eye level. There wasn't much else to do but accommodate. Contorted movements were punctuated by moans and gasps. For the rest of the evening, the cocktail dress lay in a heap on the floor.

The next morning, she couldn't remember much — except for Sherri's breasts — soft, round and sensuous, staring her in the face. For six months they were lovers on and off, a semi-casual affair that had little to do with emotional attachment. But the experience christened her desires, anchored her sexuality, affirmed her feministic sensibilities. It also taught her the value of doing good deeds.

The cloud of her life had lifted, and only a chalky white film was left hovering before her eyes. Shadows migrated across semi-consciousness, gray images that emitted a muffled kind of sound she couldn't understand. She felt the urge to fight them, to make the shadows go away. She wasn't finished looking at her life. There was so much more to see. But the present called to her, its limbs twitching, head turning from side to side. The first haze of day seeped into her vision. Muffled voices called out her name.

"Buddie. Buddie."

An olive green ceiling. Light that hurts. Aching head. Movement. I struggle to reach the voice.

"Buddie, it's Chris."

I feel a warmth on my arm and the movement becomes a face, the most welcome face in the world. Chris. I try to say her name, but the word comes out unintelligible. There's a constriction around my face I don't understand. A hissing, bubbling sound above my head distracts me. A mask strapped over my face.

"Buddie, relax. You're going to be fine."

Chris's voice is like another dream. I move my head up and down to let her know I understand, trying to comfort her as she comforts me.

"You've been sleeping a long time, Buddie. Almost two days. Do you remember the fire?"

The fire? The fire. The barn — inside as hot as a furnace. Horses screaming. Black, burning smoke. The cold night air.

"Buddie, you scared me. You scared everyone."

I raise my arm. I want to touch Chris, to make sure she's real. Chris takes my arm gently, then lays it back down on the bed. The arm is covered with bandages. I lift my other arm. From elbow to fingertips it, too, is wrapped in white bandages. Chris reads my fear.

"Both your arms were burned, Buddie. And your knee's in a cast. I talked to the doctors yesterday. With some physical therapy, everything will heal before you know it. It's your lungs they've been worrying about. But you're doing fine now."

Ignoring the bandages, I reach for her again. She

takes my arm, gently rubbing it above the elbow. Closing my eyes, I wish she would hold me.

"Buddie, I'm going to leave you for a second. Kate's in the solarium. She's been frantic. I'll be right back."

While she's gone, I take time to inspect the damage. As I look down the length of the bed, more panic. Lifting both arms, I stare at the sterile white gauze. A throbbing sensation below my right thigh diverts attention to my knee. Raising my head slightly, I see it has been immobilized and enclosed in a shiny plaster cast.

"Hey, beautiful. I knew I should've kept a closer watch on you."

Kate leans over me. She kisses my forehead, her soft skin cool against my own. Sitting on the edge of the bed, she flips the hair away from my eyes.

"I met Roger today, Liz. He was here this morning, hovering over you whenever Chris and I would get out of the way. He's crazy about you. It's something he and I have in common."

Kate pulls the covers around my waist, smoothing them out nervously. She's wearing a pale green sweater, its long sleeves pushed up to her forearms. The worry lines along her forehead seem heavier, her thin face drawn like a shriveled piece of apple. Lifting her head, Kate tries to smile. But the hollowness in her face betrays the attempt.

"I also met your mother. I don't think she likes me much. But that's okay. I'll get over it." Kate shifts uncomfortably, clearing her throat. "Liz, I want you to get your sorry ass out of this bed. And from now on, no more farms and no more barns. I'm getting too old to lose three nights sleep in a row."

Kate lays her head on my chest. As much as I can, I put my bandaged arms around her. She lets out an audible sigh, then whispers something I can barely hear. Filtering out the bubbles and hisses of the oxygen machine above my head, my mind replays her words, "Damn you, Liz. I think I've fallen in love."

Five days later I'm sitting up in bed, free of the oxygen mask and a few layers of bandages. My burns are healing, and respiratory therapy has strengthened my injured lungs. Yesterday I actually took a slow stroll up and down the hall, the hospital-issue crutches clinking noisily at my sides. My mind's ready to fly, but my body still refuses to cooperate.

"So, when are they paroling you?" a voice in the doorway asks. Kate looks more radiant than ever. "I brought you something to brighten your room." With a flourish, Kate reveals a large bouquet of spring flowers.

"Kate, they're beautiful. Thank you."

"So are you. They're a peace offering, since I haven't been here the last couple of days." Kate sits on the edge of the bed. After glancing toward the door, she leans over and kisses me. "That's how much I miss you."

For the next twenty minutes we talk, Kate's arm resting across my waist as she discusses recent events in an almost businesslike manner. She's preparing a new lecture series for the university's summer session beginning in mid-July.

"I'm doing all the prep work now because I plan to go home for two weeks at the end of June. I thought you might go with me."

"Kate, I'd love to go."

"But listen. You know my father and I don't get along. So we won't be staying at my parents house."

"I understand."

"I think I told you, my parents have a beach house at Half Moon Bay. It's a beautiful place not far from San Francisco. We can stay there. I know you'll love it."

"It's enough incentive to get me out of here — fast. Look Kate, I'm healing." Raising my arms, I show Kate the two limbs less several layers of bandages.

"Good. Soon, you'll be able to hold me again."

My mother is unusually quiet, hands folded in front of her as she clutches a purse to her lap. I'm sitting on the edge of the hospital bed, waiting for the obligatory wheelchair. Finally, after two weeks, I'm being discharged. My arms are stiff, still wrapped in gauze from wrists to elbows. The cast on my right leg is cumbersome, but in a short time I've learned the art of crutches. Getting up from the bed, I spin expertly in a circle, the crutches guiding me around my mother's chair.

"For heaven's sake, Buddie, are you trying to kill yourself again?"

"Relax, Mother. I'm just practicing."

"They certainly are taking their time, aren't they?" She looks anxiously toward the doorway. "Your father is bringing the car around. He'll wonder what happened to us."

Stretching my crutches out in front of me, I steer myself toward the window. On the edge of the sill, I notice the flowers from Kate, now withered and dry. Pulling them from their vase, I reluctantly throw them into the waste can.

"Who were those flowers from?" my mother asks.

I turn toward her, carefully weighing my answer. "From Kate. You met Kate, didn't you?"

"Oh," the curt reply comes back. "Yes, I did. It's all quite obvious to me now."

"I doubt that."

"By the way, has Roger told you of his plans?" My mother shifts nervously in her chair.

"Yes, as a matter of fact he has. Why?"

My mother looks down at her shoes. "I suppose you approve of what he's doing."

"Why wouldn't I?"

"Well, if you don't know, I'm not going to tell you."

"Good." I turn back toward the window. "Sometimes it's better to keep our opinions to ourselves. Especially in our case, since we never manage to agree on anything."

"We might agree on something, if you weren't so stubborn."

I laugh a genuine laugh, taking one giant crutch step toward my mother. "Now, that's really funny. I was just thinking the same thing about you. Maybe we're too much alike, you and I."

"Nonsense." There's indignation in her voice. "We're not at all alike."

"Whatever you say, Mother. You know best."

"I just can't believe you'd want your baby brother to throw his entire life down the drain to be a priest."

"Mother, listen to me for once, will you?" She looks at me, her eyes filled with disdain. But I also see hurt in them, so I soften my words. "Roger's a grown man. He's excited about his decision and believes in what he's doing. You should love him for it. Be proud."

"I guess I should be proud of you, too."

"Forget about me. We're talking about faith here. About dedication and commitment. Can't you see that?"

"I see two of my children throwing their lives away," she says, face set in anger and disappointment.

"Fine, fine. But don't crush Roger's spirit. If you want to take your anger out on me, go ahead. But please don't do it to him."

Stretching out on the ground next to Chris, I rest my head on the soft grass. "Well, I may just make it to California with Kate. I've still got two more physical therapy sessions, but no more crutches, thank God."

Chris runs a blade of grass across her sneaker. "You'll make it to California. I think surfing's out, though!"

"I'm such a klutz, I couldn't surf on three good legs."

Chris laughs. "That makes two of us. You hungry?"

"Starving."

Getting up, Chris extends her hand toward me. "Then, let's go poke around the refrigerator."

After lunch we sit in the yard, chairs turned to face the field and sun. Maggie sits next to me snapping at any flies that stray into our vicinity. Chris is reading a book, her dark hair blown back across her shoulders. I close my eyes, the warmth of the sun stinging my face.

"This is an active group," a voice says.

It's Bob. What a thrill, I think. He should be arrested for disturbing the peace.

"You ladies mind a little company?" he asks, sitting down next to Chris.

"No," Chris replies.

Yes, I think. He reaches over and takes Chris's hand. Any minute now, I'm sure I'll throw up.

Squinting in the sunlight, Bob turns to Chris. "Thought I might come by for a visit. Didn't think you'd have company."

"I was just leaving." I struggle to my feet, wincing as pain in my right knee shoots up my thigh.

"Buddie, you don't have to leave," Chris says, pulling at my arm. "Does she, Bob?"

Bob gets up. "Not at all. I didn't mean for it to sound that way."

"I've got to get going anyway."

"Wait, I'll walk with you to the car. Bob, I'll be right back. Buddie, you don't have to leave, you know," Chris insists.

"I really do have things to do." I open the car door, throwing my jacket across the passenger seat.

"You know, Buddie, you're so full of shit sometimes."

I turn and look at her. "Now what did I do?" I ask, throwing my hands up in disgust.

"Why don't you admit you don't like Bob, instead of being such a little shit about it? No. You'd rather make me feel guilty."

"I thought maybe you'd want some time together. Now you're pissed off at me? I'm afraid I don't understand."

"You could sit and talk with us for a few minutes. It wouldn't kill you."

I lean against the hood of my car. "Look, you're right. I can't stand the asshole, okay? And I don't feel like sitting around exchanging small talk with him." I glance at her to gauge her reaction. "There, now I've been honest. Now you can really be mad."

"Buddie, you've never even given him a chance. You don't know him. He's a nice person."

"Nice! He left you when you were sick as a dog. Now you're feeling better, and he's back."

"Buddie, I think you're jealous."

I slam my fist down on the car roof. "Jealous! Oh, that's just great. That's charming. And so what does that make you? I'll tell you what. Stupid. It makes you stupid."

"What the heck's going on over here?" Bob asks, coming down the sidewalk. Seeming to sense danger, he waits at the top step.

"Oh go to hell," I tell him, trying to maneuver my way into the car. Chris reaches out, helping me place my sore leg beneath the steering column. Our eyes meet for a brief moment before I shut the door.

I pull out of the driveway in a hurry, the wheels throwing stones onto the side lawn. Pushing down on the accelerator, I put distance between myself and feelings that may never be resolved.

Kate stands next to Chris at the kitchen stove as they each place manicotti into a baking dish.

"Are these noodles supposed to be slimy?" Kate asks with perfect seriousness.

Chris chuckles. "A little noodle slime is good for you, Kate. Lots of vitamins."

"Hey," Kate says while handing Chris another noodle. "I'm glad you two aren't fighting anymore. And over some guy to boot."

, "Kate, please," I reply from across the room. "Chris and I weren't fighting over some guy."

"I thought you told Chris you hated what's-his-name. Bob? You thought he was a bum or something. It is Bob, isn't it?"

I look at Kate with eyes that could kill. "Can we talk about something else?"

"It's okay, Buddie," Chris interrupts. "I know you think he's a jerk. Don't worry about it. After all, it's yet to be proven otherwise."

Kate snaps her fingers. "Yeah, that's what Liz said. She called him a lousy jerk. And a few other things as I recall."

"Kate, please. You're going to get me into more trouble."

Chris laughs, sliding the dish of manicotti into the oven. "I'd like to hear what else Buddie had to say. But we'll let it go this time."

"Thank you, Chris. And thank you, Kate."

Kate and Chris continue the dinner preparations. In the past weeks we've spent a lot of time together — enjoying dinners, movies, walks and shopping trips. Chris and Kate constantly tease each other. It seems to be their way of expressing what's become a comfortable friendship. I hover somewhere in between, my life filled with their laughter, comfort and love.

"So when are you whisking Buddie away to California, Kate?"

"Next Saturday. Two weeks of sun and sand. I think Liz is looking forward to it."

"It'll be a chance for Kate and I to spend some quality time together — away from the crazed pace of life around here."

"Liz hasn't had the pleasure of living with me for any extended period of time, Chris. She's in for a real eye-opener."

Chris leans against the counter smiling. "I'll bet."

"Hey," Kate says, dashing into the living room.

"This song that's on the radio right now — it's the one they keep playing at the club. Great dance music."

Kate turns up the radio and begins to dance in the kitchen doorway. I smile — she's very sexy. Even Maggie tries to join in, running circles around Kate.

Chris moves away from the stove and stands next to me at the kitchen table. "Maggie and Kate make a cute couple, don't they?"

"Not bad. They both move well."

"I've never been able to dance. I have twelve left feet."

In the doorway Kate smiles, reaching out to Chris. "Come to me, beautiful. I'll show you how it's done."

"Kate, I can't. I'm really terrible."

A hand sweeps into the kitchen, removing Chris from the room. Quickly, Chris is in Kate's arms, trying to follow Kate's movements along the living room floor. Kate slows down the pace, her hands at Chris's waist. Clutching Kate's shoulders, Chris moves awkwardly. A few minutes later she begins to catch on to Kate's instructions.

"That's it. You see, it's not that hard."

"You're good, Kate, if you can teach me how to dance."

"Dancing can be as wonderful as sex. That's what I keep telling Liz."

"Why?" Chris asks.

"Because I can't dance either," I yell from the kitchen.

The song on the radio changes from fast to slow. Kate holds Chris close, gently moving her in small circles around the center of the room. Chris follows

Kate's lead perfectly, arms wrapped around Kate's back.

"God, I like the way you dance," Kate says.

Chris laughs softly, burying her head in between Kate's shoulder and neck. "That's because I haven't stepped on your toes yet."

"You may step on whatever you like."

I stand up, moving into the kitchen doorway. "Hey, it's getting a little lonely in here."

Chris turns and looks at me. "Oh, Buddie, are you still here?"

Kate stops dead and laughs like I've never heard her laugh before. "Liz, get in here. Show us some of your stuff."

"I would if I didn't have a bum knee."

Chris smiles. "You can slow dance, can't you?"

Chris reaches out to me, and then I'm in her arms, staring into the black-brown eyes filled with a familiar softness. As I rest my head on Chris's shoulder, Kate puts her hands around my waist from behind, kissing me lightly on the neck.

"You're lucky," Kate says. "You get to dance with both of us at once."

Chris moves away, stepping aside to let Kate and I dance alone. "I better take a look at dinner. You two lovebirds can dance a while."

Locked in Kate's arms, I feel her breath along my neck. As we turn slowly to the music, I catch a glimpse of Chris watching from the kitchen. She's smiling, happy to see me happy, I think. I smile back, wanting her to know that I am.

CHAPTER SIX

"Great view, isn't it?"

Kate walks onto the porch of her parents' beach house, her chestnut eyes hidden by sunglasses. Standing beside me, she rests lazily against the porch railing. We're both dressed in the traditional California uniform — shorts and T-shirts. Kate's T-shirt bears the name of her alma mater, Stanford University.

"Have you ever seen anything so beautiful?" she asks, the wind rustling her hair like grass.

I look at her. "No, I haven't." But my answer has

a meaning of its own. "How far are we from San Francisco?"

"About twenty-five miles. I've missed this place so much." Kate leans over and kisses me. "To the beach, my love."

Kate and I sit on the beach a short distance from the water. Leaning back on our hands, we watch the seemingly endless ocean sparkling in the late day sunshine. Two waves later, the icy water reaches us, crawling up the beach to where we're seated.

"If it were possible," Kate says, rubbing my back, "I would make life stop here." Kate kisses my forehead, her hand moving through my hair. I hear her sigh; it's a sigh of resignation.

"You really miss California, don't you?"

"Very much."

"Why did you leave? Why New York? Why D.C.?"

"It doesn't matter now. I made my choices a long time ago. Besides, we're here to have fun."

Kate rises to her knees and, holding my face between her hands, kisses me again. There is a gentleness in her touch, a softness I willingly accept.

Kate pushes me down, my head hitting sand. As we kiss, the sound of the ocean seems to amplify my senses. Moving away from me, Kate takes off her shirt, shorts, underwear.

"Kate, what the hell are you doing?" Looking up at her, I shade the sun's glare with my hand.

"I'm going to make love to you on the beach."

"Kate, anybody could walk by here."

Kate bends down and kisses me softly on each

side of my neck. "This beach is private, my love. Every inch of it belongs to us right now."

Kate lies on top of me and brushes the hair from my forehead. She kisses me again, her teeth gently biting the edge of my lips. As her tongue slips inside my mouth, her hands move down to my breasts, fingers stroking my nipples. I smile, reaching out to caress her face.

"Feels good, doesn't it?" she asks, smiling back. "Just think, it gets even better."

Kate lowers her head, her tongue running across my damp T-shirt, moving lightly around each breast. Closing my eyes, I dig my fingers into the sand. Her hands are at my hips, coaxing my legs around her waist. Willingly, I comply. Whispering into my ear, she says, "Yes, I want you, too."

Kate removes my T-shirt, and then holds me tightly as the tide runs underneath us. The salt water splashes my face and Kate licks the wetness from my skin.

She runs her tongue down my neck to my chest, now free of the T-shirt. Her lips encircle a nipple. I hold her head in my hands, listening to myself sigh above the sound of the water. Gently, Kate removes my shorts, her hands moving slowly along my thighs.

"I want to touch every inch of you," she says, kissing my stomach.

I run my hands along her shoulders, skin wet and smooth. My mind is blocked with sensations. The sound of the water, the sun on my forehead, the sand beneath my back, Kate inside of me. Her hand exploring, loving me with the strength and gentleness I crave.

As my body moves to her rhythm, Kate puts her

arm beneath my neck, her tongue licking my eyelids, my cheeks, the outside of my lips. Trembling from within, I look directly into Kate's eyes and reach for her shoulder.

"Kate . . ."

"You're almost there, baby. I'm right with you," she says, quickening her motions.

My lower body rises slightly from the sand. I hold onto Kate's shoulders as the waves, inside and out, crash along the beach.

"Where do your parents live?" I ask Kate as she drives our rental car twenty miles over the speed limit — how every Californian drives, I've been told.

"On Vallejo Street in Pacific Heights. They live on the crest of a hill overlooking the bay. It's a gorgeous view."

"Sounds lovely."

As we drive through the residential areas of Pacific Heights, the view is extraordinary. The homes are large and magnificent, the land undulating and bordered by ocean blue. Finally, we turn onto Vallejo Street. A few blocks later Kate stops in front of an old Victorian mansion. I flinch when I see it, its circular tower and curved glass windows reflecting the early evening sunset. The structure's gingerbread motif of wreaths, garlands and torches contrasts with the traditional Victorian gray color. The front lawn is meticulously landscaped with yucca and century plants. Cypress trees border the perimeter. Just beyond them I see a black wrought iron fence, sculptured with grape leaf and vine.

I approach the front steps, stopping halfway up to admire the place. "Kate, it's unbelievable."

"The architecture is called Queen Anne, like some of the others we passed. A lot of these places date back to the mid-eighteen hundreds. This was my great grandfather's home."

Kate opens the front door, letting us into the central hallway around which the house is built. A large stained-glass window on the west side of the house sends multi-colored streams of light into the hallway. Directly in front of me, a beautiful wooden staircase leads to rooms above.

A tall, strikingly pretty woman greets us as we enter the living room.

"Kate, I've been waiting for you." She hugs Kate, kissing her cheek.

"Hi, Mom. How are you?"

"Fine. Is this the friend you've been telling me about in your letters?"

"That's right, Mom. This is Liz."

"Nice to meet you," I say, taking the woman's hand, surprised by the resemblance between mother and daughter.

I follow Kate and her mother to the far end of a large room decorated with late-period Victorian antiques. Kate and her mother sit down. For a brief moment I hesitate, not sure I want to sit down on anything.

"It's okay, Liz. You can sit anywhere. Even on my lap," Kate says with a wink.

I smile weakly, taking the chair to Kate's right, directly across from her mother.

"How was your trip, girls?"

"Not bad," Kate says, leaning back in her chair.

"It was great to see the beach house again. I've tried to remember the good times there."

"I haven't been there in years. Stuart's hired someone to take care of the place. He refuses to sell it, you know."

"Yes," Kate answers. "He's got some kind of fetish for the place."

Kate's mother pulls at the hem of her dress. "Honestly, Kate."

Kate and her mother trade strained glances.

"This is a beautiful house," I say, trying to break the uncomfortable silence.

"Thank you, dear." Kate's mother smiles, acknowledging the compliment. "What would you girls like to drink before dinner? I'm afraid Mr. McGowan will be late. He's been delayed at a meeting."

"What a shame," Kate quips. "We'll have a couple of beers, Mom. I'll take Liz outside."

The back of the house is a Garden of Eden, landscaped with an array of plants I don't recognize.

"Most of these plants are imported," Kate says, as if reading my thoughts. "These are yucca trees, like the ones out front, and some Australian eucalypti. Even the mosses and ferns are imported."

A stone walkway leads to a row of garden seats, small benches framed by a latticed archway. Just beyond the archway is a large white gazebo where a buffet has been arranged on two long tables.

"Is your mother expecting a lot of people?" I ask, sitting down on one of the benches.

Kate looks bewildered. "I don't know."

"Here are your drinks, girls." A soft breeze blows Mrs. McGowan's skirt as she approaches, revealing tanned legs.

Kate takes the glasses from her mother. "Thanks, Mom. Are we expecting other guests besides Dad? Or are you and Carla just trying to fatten us up?"

Kate's mother starts to say something, then looks nervously at the house. "Kate, your father is bringing some people home from the office after his meeting. It was a sudden change in plans. That's why I asked Carla to prepare extra food."

"Who's he bringing home?"

"I don't know, Kate."

"I think you do." Kate turns away from her mother. "I should've known."

Without saying another word, Kate's mother walks back to the house. Kate sits down next to me.

"Cheers," she says, lifting her glass. "To the thrill of being home."

Drinking our beers, we sit quietly as night falls over the garden. In the quiet, I can hear the rustling of the palms and the chirping of crickets. On an empty stomach the beer hits me. I glance over at the tables filled with food, lighted candles flickering beneath the platters to keep them warm. But I blink the thought of food away, my mind almost welcoming the beer's numbing effect. Kate gets up from the bench. I watch as she walks across the stone patio to the grass, stopping in front of a small shed. Kate opens the door and turns a light on, her shadow passing along the inside of the enclosure. Less than a minute later, she emerges with two more beers, twisting the caps off with the bottom of her shirt.

Seeing the look of surprise on my face, Kate explains. "There's a small refrigerator in there. My mother stocks it with beer and soda for the gardeners and workmen who take care of the property."

"Christ," I say, accepting the beer. "Life's sure rough around here."

"Yes, it is." Kate takes a long sip from her beer. "And, it's about to get rougher. Let's eat."

I get up quickly, following right behind her.

"By the time everyone gets here, we'll both be drunk," Kate says dryly. "But that may not be a bad idea."

Kate and I attack the tables of food. They are filled with antipasto salad, baked herb chicken, triple bean casserole, gingered fruit slaw, broiled salmon, vegetables baked in cheese sauce, grilled spiced hens and a host of desserts I barely glance at.

The sound of voices coming from the back of the house brings Kate to her feet. Totally unnerved, she almost drops her plate.

"Shit," she says. "The moment of truth."

I get up, too, not really knowing why. In the dim light I can see a cluster of about nine or ten people strolling toward the garden area. From the sound of the voices, they are mostly men.

Suddenly, a set of lights along the walkway and gazebo flash on, illuminating the entire garden. I notice Kate stiffen, her hand wrapped tightly around her beer. As the group draws nearer, a voice calls out.

"Where's my favorite daughter?"

"Right here," Kate answers almost timidly.

Kate's father steps from the shadows. He's a big man, well over six feet tall with dark hair graying at the temples. His face is tanned and smiling, giving him a friendly appearance. In fact, his almost placid expression puts me off guard.

"Kate, it's been a long time," her father says politely, patting Kate on the back. "Nice of you to visit."

"I've been looking forward to it." She glances past him, eyes looking left to right across the garden.

"I brought some associates from work. Hope you don't mind."

"Business is business."

"Who's this young lady?" her father asks, making his way toward me. I hold my breath and force a smile, trying to overcome my nervousness, which is really Kate's nervousness.

"This is Liz Callow. A friend from Washington."

"Hello, Liz." Stuart McGowan squeezes my hand gently. "It's always a pleasure meeting Kate's friends."

The crowd of people has gravitated toward the food. A woman I guess to be Carla brings out a cart and begins to set up a small bar. Not knowing what else to do, I sit back down on the bench.

Kate's father steps aside, turning halfway toward the shadows. "Kate, I brought an old friend to meet you."

"Oh," Kate replies with apparent nervousness. "Who might that be?"

Sensing trouble, I lean forward, watching the scene unfold. Facing his daughter, Kate's father, with a wave, summons someone from just beyond the glow of the lights. Very slowly, a tall slender woman approaches, taking the spot beside Kate's father.

"Kate, you remember Rachel."

"You knew I would."

Rachel extends her hand. "Hello, Kate. It's been too long."

"Not long enough," Kate replies coldly, ignoring Rachel's outstretched arm.

"Rachel's still working for me. She's doing a hell of a job."

Kate starts to walk away. "That doesn't surprise me. She may have hidden it for a while, but Rachel always had incredible ambition."

Staring blankly into the shadows, Kate sits down on the bench next to me. Stuart McGowan walks to the buffet table. Rachel, after hesitating for a brief moment, follows him. My eyes remain fixed on Rachel. Who is she? Who was she in Kate's life?

With the body of a model, Rachel glides like silk along the buffet table. Her tailored white suit clings just enough to reveal all the right curves — tall and tanned with long brown hair falling well below her shoulders. It's difficult not to stare. Kate's father leans over, talking softly to Rachel. She laughs, grabbing his sleeve, her long hair falling against his suit coat.

"Where's your Mom?" I ask Kate, suddenly aware that she's been missing ever since she brought our drinks.

"She won't come out here now. She's probably in the kitchen, eating dinner with Carla."

"Why not?"

Getting up from the bench, Kate starts in the direction of the tool shed. "I'm going to get another beer."

I watch Kate as she crosses the garden walkway.

A few seconds later, I realize I'm not the only one watching her. Leaving the buffet table, Rachel follows Kate, stopping her outside the shed. Kate tries to brush by her, but Rachel is insistent. She grabs Kate's arm just below the elbow, initiating a heated conversation. Kate refuses eye contact, standing stiffly, her face rigid with anger. Finally, Kate looks directly at Rachel, says something and pulls away from Rachel's grasp. Their conversation grows louder until I hear Kate yell, "Look, I'm not interested. Leave me the hell alone!"

Kate's father, hearing the commotion, makes a beeline for the shed. Roughly, he pulls Rachel away, steering her back to the garden. I finish the rest of my beer, willing myself into becoming an inanimate object.

Five minutes pass and Kate doesn't return. Nervously, I get up, heading slowly for the small shed. The door is slightly ajar. Pushing it open the rest of the way, I step inside. I find Kate sitting on the floor in the corner. She's staring straight ahead at an empty wall.

"Kate, are you all right?"

"Please close the fucking door."

I close the door and sit down next to her, pulling her toward me. Kate rests her head on my shoulder. "Kate, talk to me. Who's this Rachel person?"

Sitting up, Kate reaches toward the refrigerator. "I need another drink."

Retrieving two beers, Kate hands me one and opens one for herself. She drinks it quickly and gets another. Then she tells me about Rachel.

* * * * *

Kate met Rachel in a bar she used to frequent in the Castro. When Kate first saw Rachel, she thought she was the sexiest woman she had ever seen. She had class, grace and presence. After ten minutes of exchanging friendly glances, Kate sat down next to her.

"Mind having someone to talk to?" Kate had asked, palms damp from excitement.

"Actually, I'm kind of lonely. I just moved here from San Diego."

"Then welcome to San Francisco." Kate raised her glass in a toast, and Rachel returned the salutation.

"Would you like to dance?" Rachel asked, getting up from her seat.

"I'd love to."

Kate put her arms around the softness of Rachel, wondering what kind of dream she must be having. For a year Kate had been living in the beach house alone, practicing contract law for a small firm in Palo Alto. Immersed in her work, she managed to ignore the occasional pangs of loneliness. But that night, staring at the ocean from the beach house, she felt the need to be with people. The loneliness had finally gotten the best of her, revealing itself in a way she couldn't quite rationalize.

Kate looked into Rachel's eyes, the jade-green softness of them magnetic. Here was a woman who could put an end to restlessness.

Not long after their first encounter, Kate and Rachel began dating. From the beginning it was a stormy relationship. But there was passion, and it was passion that fused the bond.

"Kate, come to bed."

"Rachel, I'm working on this case. It's important. I have to be prepared tomorrow."

"Work is always important, darling. But so am I."

"The way you're spending all my money, this case is more important right now."

"I'm beginning to think your work is the only thing that matters. I'm certainly not getting any attention."

"Work was the only thing I had before I met you."

"I'm here now."

"Rachel, please."

"As for spending money, my dear Kate, I do intend to get a job. Better than any job you've ever had."

"Fine. Maybe I'll sleep better at night."

Rachel put her arms around Kate's neck, nibbling at the tip of her ear. "If you come to bed now, my love, I'll make sure you sleep very well."

Rachel was ambitious and, finally, after six months of inactivity, that ambition turned into resolve. Well educated, Rachel wanted a high-profile career with all the money and advancement that went with it.

"Kate, I want a job in finance. I have all the qualifications. Do you think you could talk to your father? Maybe he would know of a position."

"My father? God forbid you should work for him."

"This has nothing to do with your father. It's for me, Kate. It's what I want."

In order to cement the relationship further, Kate reluctantly swallowed her pride. She turned to her father for help, selling Rachel and her qualifications as an asset to the corporate banking structure her father had built single-handedly. After six months of pleading, Kate's father finally relinquished. Stuart granted Rachel an interview and subsequently hired her as an administrator in his own office.

"It's the beginning of a promising future," Kate's father said. "You were right, Kate. She's extremely intelligent and highly motivated."

Kate and Rachel had been together for more than a year. The new job with Stuart McGowan's firm was cause for celebration. They enjoyed a special dinner together at a favorite restaurant near Fisherman's Wharf. Talking long into the night, they made plans for their future.

"I'll always love you, Kate. You're the only one who ever believed in me. I owe you so much, darling."

"You've given me everything I ever wanted." In Rachel's eyes, Kate believed she saw nothing less than gratitude and love.

Two months later, Kate came home early from work — home to the beach house, home to the peacefulness of Half Moon Bay, home to Rachel. As she pulled into the driveway, Kate noticed her father's car and it startled her. Her father never visited, never took any interest in the place. What could he possibly want?

The front door was locked, so Kate opened it. A kind of panic tore through her, a sickening premonition that was taking shape even as she entered the front door. Her father hated the beach house. He hated everything she loved. With one exception. Kate opened the bedroom door and found them there together.

"They were screwing each other like you wouldn't believe."

I turn and look at Kate in disbelief, trying to imagine the pain she must've felt. "I don't have the faintest idea of what to say."

"There's nothing to say, Liz. Rachel wanted a job with a large paycheck. After a while, she saw how she could get it. Too bad she didn't stop there." Kate rolls her eyes. "At that point in my life, Rachel was the only person I ever really cared about. My father knew that, and he didn't let the opportunity to hurt me pass him by."

"Why, Kate? Why would he want to hurt you?"

Kate ignores the question. "In a way, I admire Rachel. It took her a while to get what she wanted. In the meantime, she had a beach house on the ocean and a girlfriend who worshipped her. Not bad, huh?"

"I think it stinks. God, I'm numb to this. I thought I'd heard fucking everything."

"Let's get the hell out of here, Liz. Let's go back to the beach house and enjoy the rest of our vacation."

Walking out onto the damp grass, we take the long way up the lawn, away from the garden. We climb the short hill to the sidewalk leading to the back door steps. As we approach the door, a hand reaches out in front of me. I stop abruptly, backing up and bumping into Kate.

"You ladies leaving so soon?"

It's Kate's father, his eyes glazed over in the moonlight. "It's late," I say. "We had a long trip yesterday."

"It's not polite to leave without saying good-bye."

His large frame obstructs the doorway.

"We're leaving," Kate says, pushing in front of me. "So please get out of the way."

"We hardly had any time to talk," he replies, unmoving.

Kate is also entrenched, a hand on each hip. "There's nothing to discuss."

"I want to make absolutely certain you know the score, Kate."

"What makes you think I don't?"

Stuart McGowan leans forward, his face inches away from Kate's own, words slurring. "I can never assume you've figured out anything. After all, it was so damned easy fooling you four years ago."

He's drunk, I think. As drunk as Kate, or worse. Silently, I pray he'll just step away from the door and leave us in peace.

Kate's eyes glare with hatred. "You're despicable."

"And you're an irresponsible, reckless no-good excuse for a daughter." Stuart McGowan's form wavers a little.

"You're a fucking asshole," Kate yells, pointing her finger into his face. "Nothing will ever change that."

"Stuart, come back to the party." It's Rachel, now standing on the lower steps. "Stuart, come back to the party," she repeats. "John has some things he needs to discuss with you."

Kate's father hesitates, then turns, stumbling down the stone steps. Rachel takes his hand and they walk away, fading into the darkness in front of us.

I take a deep breath, running my hands through my hair. Kate starts to follow her father, but I quickly grab her arm.

"No, Kate. Let it go."

Kate opens the back door to the house. Taking my hand as we walk inside, Kate squeezes it gently. Behind us, I hear laughter and shouting from the yard below. The voices have a hollow, empty sound that chills me.

CHAPTER SEVEN

Lying awake early the next morning, unable to go back to sleep, I listen to the ocean running gently up the beach. Resting my arms behind my head, I stare out the window directly to my left. The fog is beginning to lift, the horizon line showing itself vibrant blue against a blue-green ocean.

Kate lies sleeping, her arms clasped to her chest. Reaching for the robe at the foot of the bed, I get up quietly, not wanting to wake her.

In the kitchen I prepare some coffee, its aroma bringing my dulled senses to life. While it's brewing,

I open the patio doors, letting the cool ocean breeze into the dining room. The beach is deserted, its rippled sand sculpted by wind and water. The smell of salt air mingles with the brewing coffee in the next room.

Resigning myself to the odyssey of another day, I return to the kitchen and spoon some sugar into my coffee. As I move into the dining room, I hear a knock at the front door. Who would visit at such an early hour?

Opening the door, I find Rachel standing before me, her long brown hair and green eyes as striking as the beach-front view.

"Is Kate in?" she asks, taking hold of the door.

"Yes." I sigh. Life with Kate has been nothing but one interruption after another. "But she's sleeping."

"Can I come in and wait for her?"

"I don't see why not." Then I think of a million reasons why not.

Like a lady-in-waiting follows a princess, I follow her into the living room. Rachel takes a seat on the couch, crossing her long thin legs in front of her. She looks around the room, her classic profile softly accepting the room's early-morning light.

Rachel removes some cigarettes from her purse. Like her, they are long and thin.

"Do you have a light?" she asks, looking up at me like I am the head maid of the bungalow.

"No," I answer, thinking of the ten disposable lighters of every conceivable color lying in the bottom drawer along the kitchen counter. Any guilt I feel quickly subsides.

I watch her as she roots through her purse, pulling out clumps of old tissues, folded papers, lipstick tubes and pens without lids from the seemingly bottomless pit. She is politely tolerant of my presence as she goes about her business searching, and I go about my business staring. Then she mumbles something about having a million errands to run. Looking up at me, she catches me gawking.

"Is something wrong?" she asks while resuming her search.

I lie. "No. I was wondering about the person who invented purses. I could never stand them, personally."

Once again, Rachel looks up at me. "Well, where do you put everything?" There is some interest in her face, the kind of interest a geologist might have for an unusual rock specimen.

"I travel light."

"Here it is."

From some unknown place within the purse, Rachel extracts what appears to be a workable lighter. She tests it first, clicking it several times. Soon the smoke from her cigarette fills the room, its acrid smell competing with the coffee for dominance.

"Are you enjoying your visit to California?" Rachel asks, blowing smoke out the side of her mouth.

"Kate's been an excellent tour guide."

Rachel swallows some more smoke. This time it exits through her nose. "Kate can be very entertaining."

"Being around her has proven to be an enlightening experience."

Rachel smiles. Legs still crossed, she leans back against the sofa, a very short pair of shorts creeping up her thighs. So little is left to the imagination.

"I'm still in love with Kate," Rachel declares while drawing slowly on her cigarette. "Just so you know."

"Thanks for the information."

"Honesty's the best policy."

"From what I've heard, you're quite an expert on that subject."

Leaning toward the coffee table, Rachel extinguishes the half-smoked cigarette. "Look, I don't want any trouble. I simply want to set things straight with Kate. There are many circumstances I could explain to you. But I'm not about to bore you with details."

"It wouldn't be the first time." I remember Cory's visit in the middle of the night. "In fact, I'm thinking of starting my own advice column."

"Then maybe you can give me some advice."

"I doubt it."

"Let's give it a try, shall we?" An irritating sarcasm coats her voice. "I'd like some advice on how I can convince Kate to come back to California where she belongs. To be close to the people who love her."

I walk over to the front window and part the curtains. I fight to maintain my composure, anger boiling just beneath the surface. "It's a beautiful morning. California is beautiful and I know Kate misses it. She considers it her home." I step back toward the sofa where Rachel sits, her tan body a contrast to the white furniture. "But memories are all she has. From what I've heard, everyone she ever loved here has let her down. If you expect her to return on some past notion of love, you've got your work cut out for you."

"Well, I've always enjoyed a challenge."

"That's true enough," a voice says. In a robe, Kate emerges wide awake from the bedroom. "Liz, do you always let uninvited guests into other people's homes?"

"Not normally."

Kate strides into the room. "What can we do for you, Rachel? Please make it fast. I prefer to eat my breakfast without feeling nauseous."

Rachel turns to look at Kate, leaning her elbow on top of the sofa. "Kate, darling, don't be so impertinent. I've come to talk."

"So, talk."

Rachel tosses her head in my direction. "Can't we have some privacy, dear?"

Feeling like a discarded card in a poker game, I head toward the balcony. "I need some fresh air anyway."

After a brief, ten-minute chat, Kate politely escorts Rachel to the door. A few minutes later, Kate joins me on the balcony, eyes wide with a kind of astonishment.

"What did she want?"

"She still loves me. Wants me to move back. She's planning to leave my father. She wants us to be together again." Kate shrugs, shoving her hands in her pockets. "That's pretty much it in a nutshell."

"What about her precious career?"

"She's accepted a job with another firm. She's going to tell my father tonight."

"That ought to go over well."

"For sure."

"What did you say to her, Kate?"

Kate flashes a wistful smile. "Rachel thinks I ran away. There are a lot of things here at home I've never resolved. I agree with that. I did run away, and there are times when I regret it."

She kisses my cheek. "But as the saying goes, the past is the past."

The imported Mexican chandelier above my head glistens. Looking at it makes me pleasantly dizzy. The beamed ceilings and hand-crafted gold mirrors accentuate the Spanish-style dining room of Alejandro's Sociedad Gastronomica, one of the most famous restaurants in San Francisco. To my left, a group of Latin men eat steaming rice and bean dishes covered with cheese. They gesture rapidly as they talk, stopping only to refill their wine glasses. The rest of the dining room is filled with couples and families.

"Hello, girls." Kate's mother sits down, her blonde hair tied back in a red silk scarf. "Hope you weren't waiting long."

Kate, just returning from the bar, smiles sweetly. "No, Mom. Enjoying a drink until you got here. How are you?"

"Fine, dear. It was a quiet day for a change."

"Hungry?"

"Oh, yes. This is my favorite restaurant. Stuart used to bring me here all the time."

During dinner we're all quiet. No one seems to know what to say.

"I want to apologize to you girls about the other

night," Kate's mother says, finally breaking the silence. She stares at her food, her elegant face betraying helplessness. "I should've stopped what was happening, but I couldn't. I haven't been able to stop it for the last twenty years, so I shouldn't be shocked at failing again."

"You're being very hard on yourself, Mom." Kate takes her mother's hand. "Dad's behavior isn't your responsibility. It's his."

"Yes and no. Ever since the accident . . ."

"Let's not talk about the accident," Kate says firmly. "I can't stomach it right now."

"Accident?" I'm totally confused.

"You didn't tell Liz about the accident?" her mother asks with surprise.

"I wasn't sure it was necessary."

"It explains a great deal, Kate. About your father."

Kate slams her fork down on the table. "Nothing can explain away his behavior, and that's what you're trying to do."

"Forget it," I say, leaning toward Kate. She ignores me.

"Kate doesn't want to talk about it because she blames herself, because she's foolish enough to believe her father who's also a fool. Neither one of them can understand that what happened was no one's fault. It just happened."

"Mother, please. Let it rest."

"Liz is part of your life now. She has a right to know."

"Fine," Kate says, turning sideways from the table. "Go ahead. Ruin dinner."

"No, Kate. You're right. It's not for me to talk

about. I'm sorry." Kate's mother looks at me. "But I want Liz to understand that your father wasn't always this way. He was a good man when I met him. I still believe he's a good man."

"God, Mother, you're unbelievable! You can rationalize anything!"

"Kathryn Anne, that's not true. I just understand the pain of this family." Mrs. McGowan's eyes are immediately sad. "But it's a shame the pain turned out to be so destructive for everyone involved. Every day I pray it could've been different."

"So do I," Kate says. "But it's been taken to the point of vindictiveness and hatred. Some families come together. Others tear themselves apart. We are supreme examples of the latter."

"I suppose so," her mother replies. "And I'm as guilty as anyone. For letting it happen. For letting it continue until it was too late."

Two days later, in the black of the night, I sit on the outside balcony at the beach house. It's near midnight and I can't sleep. The air is cool and I shiver, wrapping my arms around my chest. Then Kate is here, standing in the doorway holding a blanket. She walks over and sits down next to me, placing the blanket across the two chairs. I pull it over my shoulders, listening as the water rolls and collapses heavily on the beach. The water is blacker than the night, a heavy moving blackness swallowing the white sand. Kate feels for my hand underneath the blanket. She clasps it firmly, placing it on her thigh.

"Beautiful night, isn't it?" she asks. "Why sleep when we can enjoy this?"

"I kept hearing the ocean while I was in bed. Coming out here seemed like the thing to do."

"I came out here because I want to talk to you, Liz. About what my mother said at dinner the other night."

"Kate, you don't have to tell me anything. I respect your privacy."

"That's why I want to tell you. Everyone else I've ever been with has always pressured me. 'What's the matter with you, Kate? Why are you so distant, Kate? Why don't you share your whole goddamn life with me, Kate?' Sometimes, there are things too painful to tell."

"You've a right to your own silence."

"I've been silent long enough."

A muffled sound, barely heard over the water, makes me turn in my chair toward the side of the house.

"Did you hear that, Kate?"

"What the hell was it?"

We listen to the silence. The sound is not heard again.

"Maybe the wind," I offer, for lack of anything better.

A few seconds later, a much louder sound splits the solitude. Kate gets up, leaning over the balcony, looking along the beach below.

"I definitely heard something this time," Kate says, walking to the far end of the porch. She scans the darkness in front of her. "What the hell?"

Kate taps the railing nervously with her fingers. Then a shadow catches my attention.

"Kate, over here."

Kate hurries back to where I'm sitting. Looking along the beach, we notice the shadow of a person walking in the direction of the house.

"Shit," Kate says, bending down toward the sliding glass door. She reaches inside, flipping off the living room light. The house is dark now, my eyes struggling to focus on the shadowy figure below.

"Who is it, Kate?"

"I think it's my father."

A burst of fear goes through me, my legs instantly numb. "He's holding something, Kate. What the hell is it?"

"Looks like a shotgun. Sit still. Don't move. Thank God he doesn't have a key to this place."

"Of course he's got a key," I say, wanting desperately to get up. My feet are stuck to the floor.

"I had Mom change the locks before we came."

I can't believe what I'm hearing. "Why?"

"You can ask that now? Look at him. He's nuts. I knew there'd be trouble. I should never have asked you on this trip."

"Well, you did and here we are. Now what?"

"We wait. If he starts for the balcony steps, we run inside, out the front door and to the car."

I watch the shadow of her father drawing nearer, his body shifting and staggering across the sand.

"Kate, he's drunk."

About thirty feet from the balcony, Kate's father stops, his face dimly outlined by a spotlight on that side of the house. A piercing explosion rips through the night air, a flash of light trailing from the gun Kate's father holds perpendicular to the ground. My heart stops.

"Kate, I know you're up there! Come out, damnit! I want to talk to you." His words are followed by another shotgun blast.

Getting up, I wobble toward the door. "Kate, he's going to kill us."

Kate says nothing. I turn to watch her father reloading the gun, his body swaying as he struggles with the shells.

"Come inside, Kate! Let's get the hell out of here, for God's sake!"

"You go inside. If he wants to talk, I'll talk."

"You're as crazy as he is. He'll shoot you!" I reach out, tugging at Kate's jacket. "Kate, please!"

She pulls away from me. "I'm up here!" Kate yells, waving her arms in the air. "So shoot me, why don't you? It'll be far less painful than anything else you've ever done to me!"

I run into the house, leaving the door open so Kate can get inside quickly. Lunging for the phone, I dial 911, my hands shaking so badly I can barely hold onto the receiver. Another shotgun blast sends me to the floor. The only thing missing is a trench, I think, trying to humor myself when all I really want to do is cry. First the fire in the barn, now this.

"Nine-one-one. What's your emergency, please?"

Two shotgun blasts later, I'm giving the details. The police are on their way. I hang up the phone and crawl toward the porch door. Kate's still outside, yelling back and forth to her father. It's a heated exchange that chills my heart with fear.

"You killed him!" Kate's father yells, his drunken voice rasping over the sound of the ocean. "Why'd you have to do it?"

"It was an accident! You know it was. Why can't

you accept that, Dad? Why can't you leave me alone?"

"You could've saved him, but you panicked! You let him die. You took my life away from me. My life!"

"He was a part of my life, too. He was my brother. My friend."

"He was my son!"

Peering between the porch railings, I watch Kate's father, his figure clearer to me now, the spotlight from the side of the house shining directly on him. My stomach curls inside as he raises the gun again. But this time, he doesn't raise it in the air. Instead, he points it in the direction of Kate, arms swaying from side to side.

"Go ahead and shoot me," Kate offers. "At least it'll be fucking over with."

"Kate, no!" I call out to her as the gun fires again. I close my eyes and cover my head, the sound of shattering glass resounding throughout the house. Shaking with fear, I wait a few seconds, the echo of the blast slowly fading. The continued silence finally brings me to my feet.

As I stoop in front of the doorway, I see Kate. She's standing unharmed, hands over her ears, elbows leaning against the porch railing. The kitchen window is shattered, shards of glass scattered throughout the small room, some stuck into the walls. And on the beach, where he had stood moments before, Kate's father lies flat on his back, clutching a shoulder and crying out in pain. The gun's next to him, half buried in the sand.

I stand up and slide the door fully open, my legs

shaking, my heart still racing. "Kate, come inside. Please."

Kate turns and looks at me, her face devoid of any emotion. "I've got to go down to my father."

I step outside, hanging onto the porch railing with both hands, watching Kate as she walks toward the recumbent man. She picks up the gun and returns to the porch, handing me the weapon. Without a word, I place it inside the door. Police sirens in the distance take me away from the scene below. Slowly, I go to meet them.

"Kate," I say quietly as I sit down next to her. "Why don't you come inside now? I called your mother. She's going to meet your father at the hospital."

"I can't come inside."

"Why?"

"I can't get up."

"I'll help you, Kate. Take my hand."

"I just want to sit here."

"Are you cold? Do you need a blanket?"

"I can't feel anything."

Sitting behind her, I pull Kate toward me, wrapping my legs around her. I put my arms around her waist, resting my head on her shoulder.

"I killed my brother."

"What happened, Kate?"

"It was a boating accident. We were water skiing. David was on the skis and I was driving the boat. He was fifteen, and I was eighteen. Like you and

Roger, we were best friends." Kate's voice breaks and I tighten my grip around her waist. "I got up some speed, and David was sailing along — he was a good skier. A damn good skier. We were both laughing, having a great time. Then I saw a boat coming toward us. It wasn't slowing down, and it wasn't changing direction. I turned the wheel to the right and reached for the gear shift. But instead of downshifting one gear, I stalled the boat and the engine cut off. I heard my brother call out my name, then I heard a thud, a sickening sound I'll never forget."

Kate gets up and walks down toward the water. I follow her. As she continues to talk, her words come faster, strung together in relived panic.

"As I turned to answer my brother's cry, his water ski hit me flush in the right shoulder. The force sent me to the floor of the boat. I got up. My shoulder was throbbing, heart pounding. I couldn't see David anywhere."

Kate begins to pace along the beach, almost shouting at the ocean, her arms outstretched and rigid.

"There was a stillness, and I thought, 'No, God. Please don't do this to me. Please don't.' But there was only the sound of water lapping the side of the boat. Then I saw the tow rope. I pulled, but there was no weight on the end. It came out of the water, cut short and clear through."

Kate turns to me, head down, arms limp at her sides. "I didn't know what to do, Liz. Then I jumped in the water. I think I wanted to die, too. I must've gone underwater a hundred times. Then, finally, when I thought I couldn't move anymore, I swam underneath the boat and bumped into him."

I approach Kate, but she backs away, tears streaming down her face. "When I turned the boat and downshifted, David's speed and momentum carried him outward to the left. He hit the second boat head on. That boat kept going. Never even fucking stopped."

Kate kicks at the sand, fists clenched in front of her. "David got tangled in the tow rope. The rope got caught in the motor and pulled him under the boat, wrapping itself around him like a mummy. When I found him, he was dead, Liz. His eyes were wide open."

"God, Kate — I'm so sorry." I put my arms around her.

"It took me a long time to pull him into the boat. Then I went to the marina and called the police. My collarbone was broken, so they took me to the hospital. An hour later, my father arrived. And that was the beginning of the end, for both of us."

Kate, still very agitated, pulls away from me again, her tired eyes searching the water. "Thousands of times I've replayed those seconds in my mind. Each time I reach the same conclusion."

"Tell me."

"It was my fault."

"Sounds more like your father's conclusion than your own."

"That's the remarkable part about it. It's the only time my father and I've ever agreed on anything." Kate turns her back toward me. "I'm going to stay out here a while longer. You go on to bed."

I leave Kate alone on the beach. In bed and half asleep, I stare into the blackness of the room. In my tired stupor, I hear what I think is a voice crying out.

Filtering in from the shore, the voice seems to wail above the ocean, "David! David!"

CHAPTER EIGHT

The month of July has been setting new warm-weather records for D.C. Today's high, ninety-five degrees, makes Chris's already warm kitchen even more uncomfortable. I watch Chris as she cooks, hands moving expertly, slicing vegetables for a salad. Her presence is comforting.

For the past hour I've been relating the highlights of the San Francisco trip to Chris who, with dumbfounded amazement, has listened quietly throughout the entire story.

"I can't believe what she's been through, Buddie." Chris places two chicken breasts in a baking dish. "How did you manage to survive the trip?"

"I hung on to Kate for dear life."

"What happened to her father?"

"Well, in addition to busting up his shoulder, he was fined for possession and firing of a weapon without a license. Kate didn't press any other charges. Guess she thought enough was enough."

"And what about Rachel?"

"I don't think we've heard the last of her. How's Bob?" I ask politely.

Chris smiles. "It's so nice of you to ask, Buddie. I know how close you and Bob are."

"How is the creep?"

Chris laughs. "That's more like it. I haven't seen him in two weeks."

"Why not?"

"We had a falling out. Although I hate to admit it, I think you're right, Buddie. He is a bit of a creep."

Chris and I sit for a moment and look at each other. Finally she smiles, and I return the sentiment.

Reaching out in the darkness, I find Kate's hand and turn over, resting my head on her chest.

Kate draws a long breath and sighs. "I hope I haven't been keeping you awake. I know I've been tossing and turning."

"I'm sorry you can't sleep."

"My mind won't stop. I close my eyes, try to relax. But then my mind starts racing again."

"What're you thinking about?"

"That maybe it's time to stop running."

"How can I help you, Kate?"

"That's just it, Liz — you can't help me. There's not a quick fix to this thing. I regret inviting you on the trip, because now you know. And while my problems are eating away at me, they're eating away at you, too. That bothers me. Really bothers me."

"We can work through these problems together, Kate."

Kate gets out of bed and walks toward the window. I watch the outline of her, rigid in the darkness.

"You're a different person, Liz. You can see the good in most things. I search for the good in everything and can never find it."

"What're you trying to say?"

"That I'm going to go on searching for something you've already found. I'm not the kind of person you can put rose-colored glasses on. I see the black and white of everything."

"Like your father?"

"My father? I'm not anything like him."

"I thought you told me once that he sees everything in black and white."

Silence settles in the room for several minutes until the words come back in quiet indignation. "That's true. But there's a difference. My father sees things in black and white because he wants to. I don't know any other way."

Swinging my chair around, I open my office door

to the main press room. "Doug, can you come in here for a minute?"

"What's up?"

"The city council's meeting tonight to unveil a multi-million dollar housing project. I've got some of the details. People will be interested to hear what the mayor has to say. Try to get an interview."

Doug takes the paper from my hand. He reads it and shakes his head, looking up in disgust. "When can I start picking my own assignments?"

For eight months Doug has been a thorn in my side, and I have placated him, trying to achieve his cooperation and respect. Recently out of college, he has no prior news experience, not even on a student newspaper. So far, I've failed to understand his obvious feelings of superiority.

"This is an excellent assignment. To be honest, I should pick someone more experienced to handle it."

Doug sneers. "Well, if you think someone else should do it — then here."

Doug holds out the piece of paper. I ignore it. "I know you can handle it. What's the problem?"

"I'm only doing this job until I find something better."

"That's too bad. You're getting excellent experience here. Look, do you want the assignment or not?"

"You think you're something, don't you?" Doug asks, wadding the sheet into a little ball. "Well, I know all about you."

"You're treading on thin ice." I meet his gaze and get up from my chair. "I repeat. Do you want the assignment or not?"

"Lucky for you, I haven't got anything better to

do." Doug opens the door to leave, then mumbles something under his breath.

"What did you say?"

"Fucking queer. That's what I said. What're you going to do about it?"

"Who the hell do you think you are?"

"Smart enough to have figured you out."

"You're fired." The words leap from my mouth before I can stop them. I push Doug out of the way. "Pat, come in here, please."

Pat sidesteps Doug and enters the office. "Is there a problem?" she asks. The tension in the room is thick.

"I need you to cover the news conference at City Hall tonight. Can you do it?"

"But I thought Doug was going."

"No. He's not."

"You haven't heard the last of me," Doug butts in. "You're going to wish you never fired me."

The door slams behind him and Pat stares at me in disbelief. "You fired him? Christ, Liz. Why?"

"Because I'm sick of his shit. He bitched about taking the assignment. Then he made some derogatory statements."

"Like what?"

"Never mind. I better let Harry know what happened. Can you take over for a while?"

"Harry's going to be pissed. Doug is one of his friends' kids."

"I know. Shit."

Harry blinks twice, then takes off his glasses,

placing them on the desk in front of him. "You fired Dougie? Why?"

"He refused an assignment," I say dryly. "And he made a remark that was totally uncalled for."

"What did he say?"

"He, uh, he called me a 'fucking queer.' "

"A what?" Harry asks, leaning over the desk.

Thrilled to have to repeat the remark again, I try to say it louder without choking. "A 'fucking queer.' "

"Damn. I knew that kid was a brat, but that takes the cake. Buddie, you did the right thing as far as I'm concerned."

Astounded, I can't move or say anything. "Thanks, Harry," I finally hear myself mumble.

"You know I'll always support you, Buddie. Always."

Two weeks later Doug is back working at the station, but in another capacity. He has been hired as an on-air personality for the AM station. Every once in a while he passes me in the hallway and smiles a cocky smile I want to slap from his face. But then I remember the words, "I'll always support you, Buddie." And I keep right on going.

As I pull in front of Kate's house, she's already outside waiting for me. Getting up from the front steps, she walks quickly to the car. I lean down over the steering wheel and smile at her, but her eyes are fixed straight ahead, missing my attempt to greet her.

Once she's in the car, I kiss her on the cheek. "Great day for a picnic."

"If you like picnics."

"Would you rather do something else?"

"The only reason I'm going is because it's a fund-raiser for AIDS. Other than that, I've very little interest."

"Then we'll make the best of it."

Pulling away from the house, I feel a chill pass through me, the kind of chill that touches every nerve. Outside, it's ninety degrees.

"Kate, I think we need to talk."

"About what?"

"About what's happening between us."

"Don't you know? We're lovers," she says with a wink, showing a momentary flash of her old self.

"Kate, ever since the —"

"Ever since the goddamn trip . . . I've been what? Different?"

"Different may not be a strong enough word."

"My father tried to shoot me, for crying out loud! How do you think I should be acting?"

"I'm worried about you."

"Sounds to me like you're more worried about yourself."

"I'm sorry if I gave that impression."

"What happened to the Liz who ran into the burning barn? The Liz with compassion and understanding? The Liz who wasn't going to choke every last feeling from my gut!"

"She's still here. Sitting right next to you."

The remainder of the trip is made in silence.

129

When we reach the picnic grove, the parking area is jammed with cars. Driving to the end of the field, I find a space in the last two rows. AIDS, it seems, has touched everyone.

"Kate, I'm going to get a beer. Want one?"

"No. But help yourself."

Kate walks off in the direction of the food. I watch her as she takes a seat at a table with a group of her friends.

Deciding not to intrude, I locate a shady spot near the softball field, sitting down to drink my beer and watch the game in progress. On the right side of the field a rooting section has taken up residence, screaming or booing whenever an interesting play occurs.

A few minutes later, a small woman steps up to the plate, unleashes a mighty first swing and smashes the ball over the outfield until it lands, to my utter surprise, about three yards in front of me. Rolling, it stops short — approximately two inches from my sneaker.

Not wanting to interfere, I ignore the ball and take a sip from my beer. Two seconds later I'm face down on the grass, my beer running across the ground in front of me. Sitting on top of my legs is the woman who had been playing center field. In her zeal to scoop up the ball she'd slipped and landed on top of me. Amidst laughter and cheers, the woman gets up. Then her hand is on my shoulder, helping me back to a sitting position.

"Gosh, I'm really sorry," she says as I look up at her. It's not a face I recognize.

"I think the runner scored."

"That's what I get for taking my eye off the ball."

She's a tall woman of medium build with jet black hair and a gentle face. Her eyes are like the day's sky — a pale, icy blue.

The woman stoops in front of me. "When I saw you sitting here, I forgot all about the ball."

Her short-sleeved shirt is unbuttoned to a point just above her breastbone. Her skin, tanned and curving at the top of each breast, glistens from the heat.

"I hope, after the game I mean, that you'll let me get you another beer," she offers with a smile.

"That'd be fine."

The table where Kate sits is full, but I stop anyway and place my plate next to Kate's elbow. When JoAnne sees me, she gets up, pointing to her own seat.

"No thanks, JoAnne. I'll find another seat." I turn to look at Kate, but she ignores me, continuing a conversation with the person next to her. I look at JoAnne and shrug. Seeing an empty table at the far end of the pavilion, I pick up my plate and start in that direction. JoAnne trails behind me.

"What's with old sour puss today?" JoAnne asks, sitting down across from me. "You two have a fight or something?"

"I'm not sure."

"Kate's been moody as hell ever since she got back from California. What in the world happened on that trip?"

"Didn't she tell you?"

"She hasn't said 'boo' since she returned. But I knew something was up — as soon as that woman started calling her again."

"What woman?" I ask, nearly choking on a piece of lettuce.

"Rachel. Kate's old love. She's been calling Kate every damn day. Personally, I don't like it. And I don't care if Kate hates me for telling you."

JoAnne reaches out and squeezes my hand, cracking every knuckle. I wince, trying to turn the pain into a smile. "I appreciate your concern, JoAnne. And the information."

"Do you think Rachel's trying to get Kate to come back to her?"

"That'd be my guess."

"I take it they ran into each other while Kate was home."

"Like two speeding freight trains."

"What's this Rachel like?"

"She's absolutely beautiful. Not a mole out of place. Smart and ambitious, too. If she didn't have such a selfish streak, she'd be hard to dislike."

"What're you going to do, Liz?"

"That's entirely up to Kate."

After lunch, the entertainment committee kicks into action. The line-up, according to the lime green posters hanging in several locations, includes an a cappella male trio, a solo female guitar player, a local rap group and a drag queen lip-synch finale. The small bandshell and stage area is located next to the volleyball court. Benches have been set up to accommodate the audience and people are already taking their seats. Sitting in the middle of the back row, I stretch my arms across the top of the bench trying to think of anything but Kate. Unfortunately, this is like trying not to breathe.

"Here's the beer I promised you. Mind if I sit down?"

Before I can answer, the dark-haired blue-eyed center fielder from earlier plops herself down next to me, a few strands of her soft hair falling across my arm. She smiles and crosses her legs, forehead still beaded with perspiration.

"I'm Sharon Grant — the one who sat on you earlier."

"Nice to meet you off the playing field. Liz Callow."

"The news announcer?"

"One and the same. I assume softball is a diversion from your primary occupation."

"Yes. Good thing, too — isn't it?" Sharon laughs, mimicking a slide much like the one that literally brought us together. "I'm a musician with the National Symphony Orchestra."

"That's great! What do you play?"

"Cello." She clears her throat and throws her arm across the top of the bench behind me. "Doing anything after the picnic?"

"Why? Do you want to serenade me?"

Sharon smiles. "Maybe."

"Excuse me. Hope I'm not interrupting." Kate's standing there, arms folded in front of her, a bemused look on her face.

"Kate. This is Sharon. We met during the softball game."

"That's nice. Liz, I'm getting a ride back with JoAnne. A bunch of us are going out tonight. Will you be joining us?"

"What time?"

"Around nine-thirty. At Dakota."

"Will you pick me up?"

"I'll meet you there if that's okay."

"Whatever. See you later."

Kate turns and saunters off, hands thrust into her pockets. Sharon removes her arm from the back of the bench. "Is Kate your lover?"

"Yes."

"Sorry, I didn't know." She glances back in Kate's direction. "Is she always so charming?"

"Actually, she's quite charming when she wants to be. She's been under a lot of pressure lately."

"Something tells me you have been, too."

"Yes, I have."

The Dakota is gray-blue with cigarette smoke when I enter, clouds of exhaled tobacco layered wave upon wave from floor to ceiling. Kate and the others haven't arrived yet, so I grab a seat at the bar.

Around nine-thirty Kate strolls in with five others, including JoAnne. JoAnne is the first one to greet me, her arms poised for a hug. I summon my courage and wait for the impending crush.

"Hi, sweetie," she says, arms enveloping me like pythons. I escape with only a bruised rib or two.

Kate is directly behind her. She is dressed in a

white long-sleeved blouse, collar up — and dark, gray cotton slacks immaculately pressed. She seems to stiffen when I hug her, a soft scent of perfume lingering in the air. "I've been waiting for you."

"I told you nine-thirty. But you were early, right?"

"A little bit."

"Jesus. Liz. Why can't you just arrive on time? Why must you always be early?" Kate throws her jacket over the seat next to me.

"Kate, if you're going to be nasty to me all evening, I'll be on my way." I get up from my chair.

"Sit down. I'll amuse myself elsewhere."

"Whatever makes you happy, Kate." I try to even out my voice, not wanting her to know how hurt I am.

Kate joins some people I don't recognize at the other end of the bar. I resign myself to an evening of solitude. Ordering another beer, I attempt to sort through the disintegrating relationship.

Without any subtlety at all, Kate's pushing me away. And the end is coming more quickly than I'd ever imagined. I drown the choking lump in my throat with a mouthful of beer. Thinking back, I try to remember the passion, the laughter, the assurance that was Kate. I wonder if this is what happens to love when it becomes familiar and painful and indiscreet. Eleven months of memories are already taking their place in my past, and I can find no means to stop the inevitable.

In a way, I welcome the end, the relief, the letting go. I'm alone, but not without composure. Hearing Kate's laughter, I wonder how long the bravado will last.

"Can I join you?"

I turn to find Sharon sitting to my left. She smiles and sits down, her long legs sliding over the stool, khaki slacks and short-sleeved rugby shirt underscoring her natural attractiveness. "Thought you might need some company tonight." She takes a pack of Marlboro Lights from her pocket. "Mind if I smoke?"

"No. This is a pleasant surprise."

"I hoped it would be."

As the crowds begin to swell with the ranks of the late night regulars, the music starts. Always the center of attention, Kate's busy dancing and socializing with her friends. It seems that nobody can take their eyes off her, a fate with which I can still identify.

"Would you like to dance?" Sharon asks.

I rest my head on Sharon's shoulder as her hands move down to each side of my waist. The warmth of her neck radiates along the side of my face, her cotton shirt brushing softly against my chin.

"Are you and Kate going to make it?"

"I don't think so."

"I'm sorry. I just lost someone, too. After six years."

I put my arms around her, hugging her tightly. "Six years is a long time to love someone."

"That's why it's so devastating. Almost like dying. Until you meet someone new and find the missing pieces."

On the way home from the club a steady rain

begins to fall, the wiper blades slashing rhythmically across the windshield. I try not to think about what I'm doing, watching the road in a kind of hypnotic state only possible due to years of repeating the same route time and time again.

I park the car in the driveway behind the apartment building, fallen branches crackling beneath tires. Unlocking the back door, we pass through the narrow hallway to the second door which leads upstairs. It's dark and quiet as we cross the living room, turn the corner and go into the bedroom. Streams of harsh light spray into the room from the outside street lamp. I draw the shades to blacken the room — matching the surroundings to my mood.

I can hear her undressing, shoes dropping to the floor. The rattle of change in a pocket . . . a watch being placed on the dresser . . . the creak of an antique bed. These are the sounds I think I must remember.

There is a hesitation in my heart as I stand alongside the bed, a hesitation that comes from knowing where things are, and where they must go. A resistance to begin what will surely end long before I would have it end. I reach for the covers and find her hand, its warmth a sudden shock to such cold thoughts. The hand closes around my own, pulling me under covers until I find her total warmth — a horizontal line I sink into. A hand takes my face and turns it gently toward a kiss, the kind of kiss that wants to be first instead of last. I linger beneath it, raising my hands to the softness of hair above the eyes I had watched earlier that day. Eyes that can guide a kiss even in the darkness. I hold the kiss in my hands, steadying the memory.

And then there are the thousand touches of love. I count each one separately. The wrapping of legs . . . touching of breasts . . . strong lingering caresses where hands and fingers and tongues form an intimate connection. Soft cries . . . whispered words . . . exhalations . . . gentle kisses all counted and remembered, as seconds turn into minutes, then hours. There are the after-moments I remember, too . . . the beating of a heart . . . the changing of minutes on a digital clock . . . rustling of sheets . . . the clasp of a hand. Over now, but remembered.

"I guess you know that I'm going back to California."

"When will you leave?"

"A week from tomorrow."

"Will you be coming back?"

"I don't know."

The ending is now as real as the one I'd embraced earlier that evening. The emotional end, the physical end, have been quietly understood and accepted by both of us. I blink, frantically trying to control the stinging sensations that quickly become tears. How easy it had been, from the opposite side of a dark, smoky room, to relinquish Kate's love. But she's the warmth lying next to me now. I try to swallow but choke instead — accidentally sputtering sounds meant to be silent.

"Now, Liz — no tears. It won't help us get through this."

I slide upward, closer to Kate's face, lightly kissing her cheek. As I do, the warm and salty taste of her own tears melts across my lips.

CHAPTER NINE

It's the end of July and Kate's been gone for two weeks. Since her return to California, there's been no contact between us. Little things remind me of her . . . a dance song on the radio, a sunset the color of her eyes, a gathering of people we knew at a place we experienced together. Sometimes, in a recurring dream, I'm looking for Kate but can't find her. In others, I call her on the phone but the calls are never completed. My fingers keep misdialing the number. Closing my eyes to the memories, I try also to forget the dreams. Dreams of Kate are as elusive as she was, and as temporary as our time together.

It seems a strange thing to find solitude in a busy downtown restaurant. But it's something I've always been able to do. The more people around me, the more solitude I find. I signal the bartender for another beer.

"If you don't mind, I'll have one."

I turn in my chair to find Sharon with the wild blue eyes. My number one softball player, and the National Symphony Orchestra's number two cellist. I change my order to two beers instead of one.

Sharon sits down next to me, her calf-length blue dress draped lightly across the chair. A thin, gold necklace flatters her long neck and wide shoulders.

"How was tonight's performance?"

"Fine — considering it was only a warm-up. We still have a few weeks to get ready for the fall schedule. It's our busiest season of the year."

"You haven't shown me your cello yet."

"It's in the back seat of my car. If you want to have a look, it can be arranged." She smiles, her dark hair an alluring contrast to the softness of her face.

"Why do I think that could be dangerous?"

After dinner, Sharon invites me to her apartment in the Cleveland Park section of the city. She offers to make some tea and disappears into the kitchen. I sit down on the sofa, taking in the room like one would peruse a flea market. Old bottles of every shape, size and color line the shelves of a wall unit across the room. Along with the bottles is a collection of pottery. Crystals hang from the shelves, the windows, the lamps — even the door knobs. I find it difficult to focus on any one spot.

"This is orange spice tea. Hope you like it."

"I'm not much of a tea drinker, but what the heck."

"Herbal tea is good for you. Very soothing."

"So what're these crystals all about?"

"Well, depending on the intensity of their electrical charges, they've got different powers. Some promote healing, some bring inner peace. I carry this one in my pocket whenever I play with the symphony. It's meant to bring life to my music."

"They've got, what did you say, electrical charges?"

"Sure. You can feel their energy. That's what they are — compressed energy. Here, I'll show you."

Sharon drops one of the crystals in my hand, closing my fingers around it. But I feel only the fading warmth of her hand pulling away. The crystal seems cold and lifeless.

"Feel anything?"

"I think it's warm in here. My hands are perspiring."

I open my hand and give the crystal back. Like a newborn infant's skin, it radiates a pale pink color. Sharon moves closer, touching my face with her fingertips.

"People also give off different levels of energy. Yours is very high."

Sharon leans over and kisses me. I let it happen, all the time wanting to hold back something not entirely finished. I end the kiss. As I pull away, instead of Kate's sunset eyes, I see the clear blue of Sharon's. In them there is a softness I cannot hold onto.

Standing up, I gravitate to a bookcase on the other side of the room. It is filled from top to bottom with books on dream interpretation, crystallography, meditation and herb lore. Scanning the titles, I try to forget the kiss. I try to forget I've got any feelings at all.

"Why don't you come back over here so I can hold you?"

"It's late. I should head home."

"Liz, are you still in love with Kate?"

"I think I need more time."

Sitting in the hospital lobby, I wait impatiently for Chris who is having her October check-up along with a stress test and echocardiogram. Since beginning the experimental heart drug, she must endure this torture once a month. I've accompanied her each time and Chris says I've become her good luck charm. But today, due to my own blue mood, I feel less charming. I feel on edge. I watch my knees as they bounce up and down in perfect rhythm with my gum-chewing. The woman sitting across from me is also watching the noticeable body language. I smile at her, but she looks away.

The hospital smells like the inside of an old

medicine bottle. Pale, green paint covers every wall and corridor.

About two hours into my wait, a short, plump nurse approaches me, her white coat a contrast to the hospital green. "Are you Buddie Callow?"

I get up. "Yes."

"Chris Bannister asked me to find you. She's still in cardiology. She'd like you to go up."

"Is everything okay?"

"She doesn't want to keep you waiting, I suspect."

I follow the nurse as she lumbers onto the elevator, off the elevator, down corridors and around corners until I realize we are following a trail of red dots on the linoleum floor. Finally, where the red dotted trail ends, we pass through a set of swinging doors into a room with draped off sections. The nurse leaves me at the middle draping on the left side of the room.

Parting the drapes, I find Chris lying on her back dressed in one of those scanty hospital gowns. An automatic blood pressure cuff is hooked up to her arm, and her chest is covered with wires and patches.

"Is it safe to come in?" I ask.

"Buddie, thank God."

Chris holds out her arms and I grab her. She's trembling, obviously frightened and upset.

"What's going on up here?"

Chris starts to cry and I start to get really scared. I close the drapes and make her lie down.

"Now, calm down. What's happening?"

"The tests weren't right, Buddie. I could hardly breathe while I was on the treadmill. And the echocardiogram took too long. It's never taken that long before." Chris tries to get up. "I've got to get out of here. Take me home, Buddie."

"Listen," I say in a calm voice. "Let's wait a little longer. Talk to the doctors. Maybe you're just tired today. It may be nothing more than that."

I wipe the tears from her cheeks. She grabs me around the waist, her hands holding me so tightly I can feel her fingernails digging into my back.

"It's okay. Everything's going to be fine. Hey, you're disconnecting here." I gently remove her arms from my waist. Two wires are dangling out of the patches designed to hold them to her chest. I snap them back into place and make her lie down. I adjust the gown to cover her, but she starts trembling again.

"Don't they have any fucking heat in this damn place? It's freezing in here," I mumble. On a stool, next to an instrument cart, I spy a folded blue sheet. I grab it, keep it doubled and throw it over her.

"Thanks, Buddie. I'm sorry. How embarrassing."

"Listen, this place is giving me the creeps, too. No wonder you're scared. How long have you been waiting here?"

"At least forty-five minutes."

"Well, I'm going to find that nurse."

Chris objects, grabbing my sleeve. "Please don't leave me."

I take her hand and hold it tightly. A half hour later we're in the car on the way home. Chris has a fistful of new prescriptions and orders to rest until she gets a consultation call from Colorado. I stay the night but don't get much sleep. My insides are raw with fear.

* * * * *

My mother lights a cigarette, smoke swirling in my direction. I crack my car window.

"Buddie, don't drive so fast."

"I'm only doing thirty-five, Mother. And stop holding onto the door."

"I will if you'll slow down."

I brake to a crawl, wondering what the people behind me are thinking.

"How's Chris? You haven't said much about her."

"The drug is beginning to lose effect."

There is a momentary silence as my mother fumbles for the car's ashtray. Glancing in her direction, I notice the pallor of her skin changing from pink to white. Her eyes close for a moment, as though she's recalling the hopelessness of similar news heard many years ago.

My mother clears her throat, wiping some stray ashes from the lap of her dress. "Buddie, I'm sorry. That's awful news."

"She's getting weak again. Short of breath. I think her spirit's faltering. We had such hope."

My mother reaches across the seat and pats my forearm. "I'm going to pray for Chris, Buddie. I'm going to pray very hard."

CHAPTER TEN

There's nothing more frenetic than a radio station just before the holidays. During the midst of this madness, Doug suddenly flies into the newsroom as though his pants are on fire. Pat and I turn, our chairs swiveling us around like marionettes.

"I'm sick and tired of the shoddy operation you two are running. I've had it!"

"Now what's your gripe?" I ask, standing up.

"I put this cart into the machine for the half-hour pre-recorded newscast, and do you know what it played? Dead air. Isn't this your cart?"

Pat reaches for the tape. "Gosh, I don't know, Liz. This could be any old cart."

"Maybe you grabbed the wrong one, Doug."

"The hell I did!"

"Or maybe you erased it to make Pat and I look bad."

"I wouldn't waste my energy. Listen, my show is perfect. You two incompetents better stop screwing it up."

"Who do you think you're talking to?" I ask, opening the door. "Get out of this office until you can learn to treat your co-workers with a little respect."

"I could never have any respect for the two of you." Doug wags his finger in front of my face. "Especially you."

Maggie nuzzles me with her nose. She licks my ear and lets out a mournful cry. We're both lonely for Chris who is in the hospital undergoing another battery of tests.

When the phone rings, I run to the kitchen, expecting a call from Chris. Maggie follows close behind, not wanting to miss any news.

"Liz, this must be my lucky day. I didn't know if you'd be at Chris's or not."

There is silence as my thoughts tumble. My mind races back to recent memories where I find the feelings still there — unchanged. "Kate, I'm surprised to hear from you."

"I meant to call before, but I couldn't bring myself to do it. I knew you'd be angry."

"I think hurt would be more accurate."

"I never meant to hurt you, Liz. I'm sorry you got caught in the middle of things. How are you?"

"Nothing much has changed."

"And Chris?"

"Not good. She's at the hospital having more tests. Then she's going back to Colorado for another consultation with the heart specialist. The drug doesn't seem to be helping anymore."

"I'm sorry. I love Chris. I wish I were there."

"I wish you were, too. It's hard for me to lose hope."

"Then don't."

"How've you been, Kate?"

"I'm beginning to straighten up the loose ends out here."

"Did things work out with Rachel?"

"Those problems have been resolved. And I've been talking with my father, too. We'll never be best buddies, but at least we're trying."

"That's good news."

"Liz, I'm sorry about us. In fact, I think about us every day. But I needed to come back here and put the pieces of my life in order. I should've done it long ago. Hope you understand."

"I'm trying to."

"I've got to get going. Promise you'll call me when you have news about Chris. Give her my love. I'll be thinking of you both."

"What time does your plane leave?" I ask as Chris packs the last of her clothing.

"Two o'clock."

I take her luggage and portable oxygen tank downstairs. Her footsteps follow me. When I turn around, she's standing behind me, only inches away. I'm fighting for composure.

"Stop it, Buddie. This isn't good-bye."

"Stop what?"

"Looking at me like I'm already dead."

"Now don't start that shit, Chris. Please."

She puts her arms around my neck, resting her head on my shoulder. I hug her as tightly as I dare; she seems so fragile.

"When I get back after the holidays I hope there's snow, because I'm going to whip your ass."

"Not likely."

She looks up at me and smiles. "You're such a shit. I don't even know why we're friends."

"Because you're crazy about me."

"You're right. I am."

I push the soft hair away from her face, kissing her on the cheek. "You do what the doctors tell you."

"Oh, they're full of shit, too. All I really need is a heart transplant."

"Chris, for God's sake. There's probably a million things they can do before that. Now, c'mon. The taxi will be here any minute."

"I'm not leaving until you kiss me properly."

"Huh?"

"Are you deaf?"

Chris throws her arms around the back of my neck and starts to kiss me. A tender, passionate kiss that makes my head swirl. Thoughts dive bomb my brain, flying by so fast I can't read any of them clearly. Except one. Please, don't leave me. I slide my arms underneath her jacket, around her back so I can really hold her. The seconds race away from me and the kiss ends, her soft lips still lingering along my neck. Then a car horn rips through the air and we look at each other helplessly.

Chris grabs hold of my coat lapels with both hands, tugging on them, face buried in my chest. "Damnit, Buddie! When . . . when I get back the first place we're going is upstairs."

There's a knock at the front door.

"Shit. Timing is everything." Chris lets go of my coat and picks up the smallest suitcase.

Reluctantly, I get the rest of Chris's luggage and follow her to the door. It's the taxi cab driver. A cigarette dangles between his lips as he barks, "Lady, you ready?"

In a daze I stagger outside, surrendering the luggage to the driver who hauls it to the car. At the bottom of the porch steps, Chris and I linger, unable to find words.

"We'll talk on the phone every day, Buddie."

"You bet."

"You'll keep Maggie company?"

"Absolutely."

"I love you."

"I love you, too."

Chris puts her hand to my face, smiles, then turns to leave. I grab her shoulder, pulling her back into my arms. We kiss again, the warmth and softness of her painfully impermanent.

"I wonder what the taxi driver's thinking?" she whispers in my ear.

"That we love each other madly, I hope."

"He'd be right."

Chris opens the car door and gets inside, the door sealing itself shut like a Tupperware container. The mustard yellow cab pulls away, tires squealing onto the street. For a long time I stand in the driveway, staring at the bluish-gray stones covering the brown earth beneath my feet. Once again I'm stuck and can't move, past fears crushing inward.

CHAPTER ELEVEN

Sharon rolls the dice — double sixes. "Well, that should do it for this game," she says with a victory smile.

"I never saw such luck. You must've rolled at least ten doubles this game."

"Luck? It's skill, Liz. Pure skill."

"Too bad you don't play softball like you play backgammon."

"Very funny. Hey, you said Chris called last night. What's happening in Denver?"

"I'm not sure."

"You seem worried."

"I'm trying not to worry." I close my eyes, recalling the conversation with Chris — stuck on some thought I can't express.

"Buddie, I miss you."

"I miss you, too. How're you feeling?"

"Just dandy."

"What did the doctors say?"

"They took most of my drugs away. Guess I'm finished with those. Seemed they were corrosive to my liver. Ha! Imagine that?"

"Your liver! Now what?"

"Not to panic. The old ticker's still ticking. It's hard to cut through all this medical bullshit. I'm getting a little sick of people in white coats staring at me."

"When will you be coming home?"

"I'm not sure. My sister and I are in quite a reminiscing mood. I keep having these weird dreams about my childhood. She's filling me in on what's fact and what's fiction."

"I'm watching over the farm and taking care of Maggie. We'll be here waiting for you."

"I've got a picture of you both next to my bed. I don't remember when it was taken, but you look like hell."

"Geez, thanks."

"You should see me right now. Talk about hell!"

"Why don't you come home and let me take care of you?"

"You've done your share, Buddie."

"Hope you know how much I love you."
"I love you, too."

Sharon reaches across the table and squeezes my shoulder. "You worry too much. Chris would be angry with you."

I look up at her. She's genuinely concerned. "I guess you're right." A weak reply that doesn't fool either one of us.

"When's Chris coming home?"

A rush of panic grips my throat in a vise-like hold. Although I'd asked Chris the same question, when posed to me it brings the thought into frightening perspective. Suddenly, my mind launches into a replay of the moments before Chris left. The image of Chris's face is so clear, the look in her eyes when she hugs me at the top of the porch steps so vivid. I see a pain I hadn't identified then. How could I've been so stupid?

Stiffening, I clutch my shoulders. I can feel my body shudder as I remember Chris saying, "This isn't good-bye." The hell it wasn't! She knew! And now I know. I'm never going to see her again.

"Liz, are you okay?" Sharon asks, holding my hand.

"Chris isn't coming home — ever."

"Of course she is."

"No. I know it now. She's not coming home."

The bell at the shop sounds, keeping tune with

the Salvation Army bell on the nearest corner. I enter Chris's studio, the warm air melting the snowflakes on my coat sleeves. The store's crowded with holiday shoppers rushing to select last-minute gifts. I look for Jean, Chris's business partner, and finally locate her in the framing workshop.

"Jean, how's it going?"

The older woman hangs several frames back on the wall display. "Hi, Buddie. Nice to see you."

"Sorry to bother you at such a bad time, Jean. It looks pretty busy around here."

"Yes, we're starting to run out of things."

"Chris'll be glad to hear that. Have you talked to her lately?"

"She called me from Denver about a week after Thanksgiving. I've been meaning to call her back. Has something happened?"

"I'm not sure. But you know me, I worry all the time."

"I can see why. It honestly broke my heart when Chris had to sell."

"Sell! Sell what?"

"The shop. She sold her interest to Jim and I at the end of October. Didn't Chris tell you?"

"You and your husband own the shop now? Oh, God — this doesn't surprise me." I pull my gloves off, slapping them down on top of the counter. "No, Chris didn't tell me."

"Chris was very worried about upsetting you."

"That's why I came to see you, Jean. I'm on a fact-finding mission."

"Come back to the office. You look like you could use a cup of coffee."

Trailing after Jean, I feel betrayed as well as

155

incredibly stupid. I wonder if these emotions are allowed. Being angry with Chris, under the circumstances, seems out of place. Awkwardly, I smile at Jean, dragging a chair over next to her desk.

"Coffee?" she asks filling her own cup.

"No, thanks. I don't think I can handle the caffeine right now. I'm already jolted. With worry."

"I can see that."

"When Chris had her final battery of tests here in D.C., did she talk to you about them?" I brace myself, not sure I want to hear the answer.

"She told Jim and I that the results weren't good. Her heart was failing again and there'd been some liver damage caused by the drugs. The prognosis on this end was very poor."

"Did they say how much time she had?"

Jean hesitates, her face lined with sadness. "Three to six months."

Mentally I count from November to April. "Thanks, Jean. I'll let you get back to work."

Beyond the seminary gates, I follow the stone sidewalk to a large arched doorway surrounded by massive columns. Inside the entrance, at a wooden desk covered with books and papers, a young priest sits writing in a notebook.

"Can I help you?"

"I'm here to see Roger Callow. I'm his sister."

"Walk through those two doors and make the first right. You'll find a small lounge. Have a seat, and I'll let Roger know you're here."

The lounge is empty. It has a musty odor — the

smell of old books. I take a seat in front of a clear, leaded glass window. From it I see a squared-off courtyard connecting this building with several others. The room is more like a library, its walls packed with hundreds of volumes. A white porcelain statue of Mary sits to my right. Her hands are stretched outward; she seems to stare at me. Feeling a non-Catholic unworthiness, I look away.

And then he's standing there perfectly erect, his hands clasped at his waist — a handsome man with a still-boyish face. His long black robe almost touches the floor, the white collar a striking contrast. I hardly recognize him, his leaf-green eyes his only betrayal. I feel so alienated from his world.

"Don't I get a hug?" Roger asks.

Without replying, I stand and wrap my arms around him, the stiff black coat brushing against my face. I'm not sure I want to let go.

"This is a nice surprise, Buddie. I've missed you."

"I've missed you, too. I thought maybe you could show me around Philadelphia. I know it's short notice, but I'm here for the weekend." I had taken the Amtrak on a whim, needing to get away from D.C. Wanting to see Roger.

"Great! We can have dinner tonight. I know this great restaurant down at Penn's Landing."

"How're they treating you?"

"Like the green seminarian that I am. Father Post says I'm so wet behind the ears I might drown."

"Pretty soon you'll be teaching them how to swim."

"Give me another six or seven years."

Roger takes my hand as we stroll into the

courtyard. A small fountain bubbles hot water, vaporizing as it mixes with the cold air.

"Do you want to tell me what's wrong, Buddie?"

He squeezes my hand and I smile. "You know me all too well."

"After twenty-eight years I should."

"It's Chris. She's gone to her sister's in Colorado. She's very sick. I just found out that she's not coming back."

He seems to comprehend immediately. He turns in front of me, his shoes scraping the pavement like sandpaper. "She went to be with her family. That's understandable. It's a hard thing to ask friends to help you face death. With family, there seems to be almost unwritten responsibility to help, but . . ." He shrugs.

"She didn't explain to me what she'd planned. What she was thinking. Not even what the doctors told her. She made me believe she was coming back."

Roger puts his arm around my back. "Can you picture that conversation, Buddie? What it would've been like? How painful it would've been for both of you?"

"She ran away."

"She went away."

"I'm pissed at her, Roger. Really pissed."

"I think you're angry at what's happening to her."

"Why? Why is it happening?"

"That's one question I can't answer, Buddie. One I'll never be able to answer, even if I read every book in this place and study here for the rest of my life."

* * * * *

After a day of hunting for post-Christmas season bargains, my mother and I have lunch at a Mexican restaurant across from the mall. We haven't had a single argument all morning — a new world's record.

As I scrape the guacamole from my taco salad, my mother raises her head, eyelids fluttering as she stares at me from across the table.

"I started a prayer chain for Chris."

I stop chewing a tomato and struggle to swallow. My mother redirects her stare back to the enchilada on her plate. "What's a prayer chain?" I ask.

Without looking up, my mother says, as if I should know, "A prayer chain is when you put someone's name in the church bulletin. The congregation prays for that person as a group and individually. We also send the name to other churches throughout the country. All of these people will pray for Chris to get well."

"Like a chain letter for someone who needs help?"

"Yes."

"It was nice of you to think of her, Mom."

My mother fidgets with her napkin, twirling it into one long strand. "I got worried when you told me Chris wasn't coming home."

"It's still hard to believe."

"Why don't you fly to Colorado to visit her?"

"I don't think it's what she wants."

"No, I agree. You know, when I heard about Chris, it took me back. It made me think about your father — how sick he was."

"It must've been hard for you."

My mother closes her eyes, then touches a lock of hair resting on her forehead. "Do you know your father's hair was completely gray when he died? He was only thirty-two. During the last few days of his life, I remember him having to lift his left arm with his right hand just so he could read his watch. I was never so frightened in my entire life."

"I don't know how you got through it alone."

"I made friends with someone in the waiting room — another young woman. Her two-year-old son was very sick. We tried to comfort each other. Even though we were strangers, that was all we needed to bring us together. But then her son got well. Your father died. Suddenly, we had nothing in common anymore. Life's funny, isn't it?"

"Sometimes it's not funny at all."

"Come here, Maggie. Your Mom wants to talk to you." I hold the phone to Maggie's ear as Chris talks. Her tail wags so hard against my leg it stings.

"I got the phone bill today," I tell Chris. "Don't even ask. I think Maggie's going have to join the work force, too."

"Have any of those calls been to California?"

"A few."

"How's Kate?"

"Good. I'm happy for her, Chris. She seems to be settling down a little."

"Kate? I find that hard to believe."

"People change."

"Yes, I know."

"Feeling okay?"

"Not bad, actually. I even managed to finish a new painting."

"Great!"

"Still angry with me?"

"No."

"You should be."

"Well, you know me — I'm pretty tolerant. Even if I do think you're a lousy shit."

"Had a dream about you the other night."

"Yeah? What about?"

"Sorry, it was x-rated."

"I'd still like to hear it."

"What about your phone bill?"

I look down at Maggie, tongue flopping and dripping saliva onto the floor. Smiling as only a dog can. "Maggie promises to look for work first thing in the morning."

"Well, then I guess we can talk a little longer."

One minute into the ten o'clock newscast, there's an equipment malfunction. A commercial begins to play over an open line, feeding into the control board and out over the airwaves as I speak. I continue reading, looking desperately for the offending tape machine. But neither one of the machines in front of me is playing. Still reading the news, I look toward the control room where Doug is waving his arms violently through the double glass. I stop reading, turning off my microphone in disgust. So much for the ten o'clock news. It's yet another fine day at the radio station.

Before I can get out of my seat, Doug runs into

the news booth. His face is bright red, eyes almost bulging from his skull.

"What the hell are you doing?" he screams, leaning into me.

I pull off my headset. "I was about to ask you the same question."

"You were supposed to break for commercial."

"That's right, but not for another thirty seconds."

"Bullshit! I know when the goddamn commercials are supposed to play! That's my job. Why don't you do yours?"

I stand up and try to walk by him. He blocks the exit. "Doug, let's not start. I'm going back to my office."

"I'm not done talking to you yet."

"Yes, I think you are." As I'm trying to push past him, he grabs my arm roughly, pulling me back into the room. "Let go of me, Doug."

"I said, I'm not done talking to you."

"If you don't take your hands off me, you're going to be sorry."

"Wrong."

Before I can react, Doug's hand collides with the right side of my face. I'm so stunned I lose my breath.

"Hey, hey! What the hell's going on in here?"

Looking up, I see Harry barge into the room. He walks over to me, nervously buttoning his suit coat. "Buddie, did I see what I thought I saw? Did Doug just hit you?"

"Yes, that's what you saw."

Harry turns toward Doug who begins to stammer

and back up. "She ruined my show, Harry. This isn't the first time. I had to teach her a lesson."

"Son, if I ever see you in this building again, you won't know what hit *you*."

"Listen to me, Harry. It's a goddamn conspiracy! She and Pat have it in for me. Ever since you hired me back."

"You have ten minutes to vacate the premises, or I call the police. You'll be lucky if Buddie doesn't decide to sue you. Out!"

Doug leaves, slamming the door behind him. I turn toward the far wall, trying to control my humiliation and anger.

"C'mon downstairs, Buddie. This is really my fault. I should never have hired that kid back."

"I'm okay. I want to get back to work."

"You take the rest of the day off. I'll go talk to Pat."

Two weeks later, a slave to routine, I walk M Street from Georgetown to the metro stop at Foggy Bottom. Pat's been on vacation all week, so I anticipate another long day at work. It's early morning, minutes before sunrise, and the streets are empty of any signs of life. Reaching the metro, I trudge down the concrete steps which lead into the tunnel. There's a cold breeze shooting through the underground. February has taken away the January freeze, but winter has refused to yield. As if to confirm that thought, I slip on a patch of ice — my feet flying out from underneath. I hit the concrete hard, letting out a low moan that echoes in the lightening shadows. Putting my hands down on either side of me, I try to push myself up. But something heavy on my chest pins me to the cold floor.

"This is too good to be true," a voice says from the shadows. "You saved me the trouble of knocking you down."

Immediately I recognize Doug's voice, his quick breaths close, hissing in my ears. "Doug, if you're trying to get revenge by scaring me, you've accomplished your task. Now let me up."

The heaviness on my chest is his knee. It digs into my breastbone, causing me to gasp.

"You shouldn't have gotten me fired. Not once, not twice."

"You shouldn't have hit me, Doug. This is a grown-up world you're in now. You've got to play by the rules."

"Play by the rules? That seems very funny, coming from you."

"Look, you've got a real chip on your shoulder. So why don't you let me up, and we can talk about it."

"You're all scum."

"You're entitled to your opinion."

"Not even worth the air you breathe."

"Doug, don't be stupid. Any minute, someone's going to come walking along here. It's getting light out."

The pressure on my chest eases slightly. "I wanted to make sure you knew how I felt about you — and what you are. And don't think there's any sad story behind it. I just hate queers, plain and simple."

"I'm sure you have company."

"Tell me you despise what you are."

"What?" I can't believe what I just heard. He's out of his mind, I think.

"Tell me you hate what you are. Admit that you're scum."

When I hear the word *scum* for the second time, anger wells up inside me, building like steam pressure from an overtaxed boiler. Suddenly, everything comes rushing forward . . . my father's death, Chris's illness, the fire in the barn, Kate leaving, my mother's bitter indifference, Doug's constant harassment . . . and now this final insult. It's too much.

With all the effort I can muster, I slide my arm from beneath Doug's weight. Before he can react, I thrust my arm forward, impacting the side of his head squarely with the heel of my hand. The shadow of him wavers for a moment, then tumbles backward hitting the cold concrete with a satisfying thud.

Not waiting another second, I get up and stand over him, feeling the rush of adrenaline. "Goddamnit, I wish I knew what your problem was. What're you afraid of, anyway?"

He blinks several times, blood trickling from his ear. "Christ, you hit me."

"Damn right. I'm sick of your shit. I'm sick of everyone's shit. If there's any scum in this subway station, I'm looking at him. Don't you ever come near me again."

I leave him lying there, dazed and bloody, taking my anger with me.

Sharon runs to answer the phone as I take the broiled fish from the oven. Placing the dish on the dining room table, I light candles to augment the mood. On my way back to the kitchen, Sharon intercepts me. "It's for you, Liz."

"Sit down and eat. Don't wait for me."

"I'll wait."

Wiping my hands on a kitchen towel, I cradle the receiver on my shoulder.

"Buddie, it's Sara Chapman. We met at Chris's New Year's party a little over a year ago. Remember?"

"Yes, of course."

"Chris gave me your number. I talked to her this evening. Wanted to tell her the news right away."

"What news?"

"Her work has been accepted for a showing at the National Museum of Women in the Arts."

Hearing the news, my throat closes up. I can barely speak. "That's . . . terrific. Best news I've heard in a long time."

"Chris gave me the list of paintings she wants to show. She has them stored at the shop with Jean. And there's a new one she's going to have her sister ship from Denver. I'm so happy for her. She worked hard for this."

"When will the showing take place?"

"The first week in April."

"Is there any way it can be sooner?"

"I'm afraid not."

"Then I'll pray for a miracle."

"I've already started."

CHAPTER TWELVE

The last day of February is cold, areas of snow scattered like patchwork on a quilt. It's late afternoon when Sharon and I pull into the driveway next to the barn, determined to catch up on the daily chores.

"I'll take care of the horses, Liz. Maggie can help. C'mon girl."

"And I'll find something to make for dinner."

In the house I poke around the freezer and refrigerator, finding enough remnants to make meatloaf and a salad. In the midst of my forage, the phone rings. With the hamburger in the microwave to defrost, I pick up the receiver.

"Buddie, this is Karen Stuart, Chris's sister."

In my heart, somewhere right next to the fear, I quietly weigh the moment.

"Buddie . . ." The voice on the other end weakens. "Chris died this morning. I've always dreaded making this call. I know how close you and Chris were."

The word *died* shoots through my head like mortar fire. My mind flashes brilliant white.

. . . With a fat stick I'd found in the backyard, I sat on the bottom porch step and beat and stabbed at the earth until the air was filled with a dirty mist. Then a shadow fell across the ground. I looked up through the brown haze into the face of a friend who lived down the block. She stared at me, her face crinkled, lips pursed.

"Hi, Buddie," came the two soft words.

I continued beating the ground, not really looking at her, not really looking away.

"My Mom told me."

"Told you what?"

My friend wrung her hands, swaying back and forth. She looked stupid in that lacy yellow Easter dress. "About your daddy."

"What did she tell you?"

"That he . . . died. I'm sorry, Buddie."

That word again. Something in me snapped. I felt my cheeks go red, my throat go tight. I was sick of hearing that word. *Died.* Why couldn't they all leave me alone?

In one swift movement I got up. The stick left my hand — flying across the yard, hitting the wooden fence with a clack. Then my right hand swung out, slapping the face of my friend.

"Don't you ever say that again," I blurted angrily.

I watched my friend's tears come, and then she ran away. Good, I thought as I retrieved my stick. I sat back down on the step and began pounding the dirt all over again.

"Chris left me a note with your name on it, Buddie. Would you like me to send it to you?"

At the sound of Karen's voice, my thoughts snap back. "Please."

"Buddie, thanks for everything you did for Chris."

"Thank you for calling."

There is a dream-like quality that overtakes me from that moment on — a disruption of space and dimension. Things seem larger than normal, my feet too big for my body. As I wander the rooms all I can think of is the time I first met Chris. Then there are dinners in the farmhouse kitchen, late-night walks down moonlit roads. There's the sound of laughter during a December snowstorm, and a New Year's Eve celebration with the promise of a "great year." The carousel of memories circles inside my head. I find myself walking out to the barn, trying to make sense of the flashing images.

* * * * *

"Buddie, don't go in there. Wait for the Fire Department!"

"If I wait, it'll be too late."

The barn door is open, a checkerboard of sunlight and shadow splayed across the dusty floor. I take a few steps forward. A woman stands sweeping dirt into a large pile.

She looks up. "Liz, are you okay? You look funny."

"This isn't the same barn."

"Liz, what's wrong?"

She steps closer into a patch of yellow light. Sharon with the death-blue eyes.

"Chris is dead."

The broom drops, skittering across the floor. "Oh, God. Liz, I'm so sorry."

The arms around me hurt. I wince and step away.

"Liz, let's go inside the house."

"Chris is dead."

In the center of the room my nephews play with their father, Steve, rumbling and tumbling like wild animals. Growls and roars, little shrieks and laughter can be heard as the jungle game continues. From the kitchen, the smell of dinner permeates the living room — roast ham, scalloped potatoes, fresh vegetables. My mother's working, the clinking and clattering of utensils and pots evidence of her activity. Lois reads a magazine, glad to be free of the kids if only for a few minutes. Roger and my stepfather watch basketball in the den.

For three weeks, thoughts of Chris have kept me company along with a kind of self-destructive lethargy. I have motioned my way through the days and nights, numb to any other feelings but emptiness. Somehow, I must follow this path of mourning to its end.

"Chris, it's still not working."

"I have it on all the way."

Shaking the hose, I watched as one drop of water fell from its opening. "Something's wrong," I said, peering into the small, round hole.

"Wait a minute. Here's the problem."

I felt a tug. Suddenly, a burst of water sprayed me in the face. Standing under a shower of water, I watched Chris, through a misty spray, approach from the side of the house.

"Buddie, I'm sorry. There was a kink in the line." She began to laugh, doubled over and crouched to the ground.

"Why do these things always happen to me?" I asked, water spraying from my lips.

"I think things just happen to us, Buddie. The combination of you and me doesn't always work."

"We'll see about that." I raced across the lawn toward Chris, hose firmly in hand. Chris, caught off guard, fell backward onto the lawn.

Knowing what I was about to do she yelled, "Buddie, don't!"

I shoved the running hose down her back. There was a mixture of screaming and teasing as the hose was tugged back and forth until we were both drenched.

Later, we rested on the lawn next to each other, dripping wet and laughing. Then I rolled over, grabbing her by the forearm. She turned her head sideways to look at me, a childlike grin on her face.

"You make me so damned happy," I said, squeezing her arm.

"You make me so damned mad," she replied. She turned away, laughing again — propping her legs up on the lower fence rail.

I didn't want to let go of her arm. I held onto it, trying desperately to hold onto her. As she laughed, she looked toward the sky, all the time tousling my hair with her fingertips, smoothing it out around my ears.

"The sun feels good, doesn't it, Buddie?"

"Everything feels good right now."

The sound of talking brings me back to the present. My stepfather and Roger have just emerged from the den.

"Is dinner ready yet?" Steve asks, looking in my direction.

"I don't know," I reply laconically.

Roger leans down and kisses my forehead. "Chin up, Buddie."

"I know. I know. Even I'm getting sick of myself."

"Buddie, can you help me with a few things?"

My mother's voice trails into the living room. Roger and I look at each other with raised eyebrows. Slowly, I get up and shuffle into the kitchen. I feel like I'm walking in my sleep.

"Buddie, can you carve the ham? You always do such a nice job."

I look at my mother sideways, wondering if I'd just heard a compliment.

"Feeling any better today?"

"The same."

My mother extends her hand. When nothing else happens, I realize she wants to hold mine. "You've got to give yourself time, Buddie. I know you're still upset about Chris. But time will help."

There seems to be genuine concern on my mother's face and, strangely enough, I understand it. Death, to my mother, is not an unfamiliar companion.

Without realizing it, I reach out to her. "I thought I'd be able to handle things, Mom. I tried to prepare myself. It didn't help, didn't make it any easier."

"It's never easy, Buddie. No matter how or when it happens."

My pathetic search for help turns suddenly ugly in my own mind. Turning my attention back to the ham, I feel myself bristling at my mother's comments. If Chris had been my lover, would her attitude be different? "Friend" has such a safe connotation.

"I wish you could've been this supportive six months ago. Or a year, or two years ago."

"We haven't been very good friends, have we?"

Placing the ham on top of the stove, I begin to search through the cabinets for the electric carving knife.

"I know it's here somewhere," I mutter, slamming the last cabinet door.

My mother hands me the knife. Looking at her, I remember the times she refused any help I might've given. She was a stranger to me then, an adversary who had put me through hell. Now, years of disappointment later, I wonder who this woman is.

"Maybe if we both try a little harder, we can start to be friends, Buddie."

A smile crosses my mother's face. I find myself searching for the real meaning of her words. Silently, I pray for the strength to empty my heart of a distrust that's nearly as old as I am.

"We could've been friends long ago — when we really needed each other. So much time's been wasted."

I begin carving, the blade moving smoothly through the ham. I layer the slices onto an oval serving platter.

My mother moves closer, removing her apron. "Does that mean it's too late to try?"

"No, of course not."

"We can take each day as it comes and see what happens."

"It's what I've wanted for a long time."

"For once, Buddie, we both want the same thing."

* * * * *

There's a touch of spring in the air Chris would've loved. The farm is beginning to flourish, its greens and yellows finally overtaking the browns and grays of winter.

It's difficult to feel the joy of new life when death has so recently demonstrated the impermanence of all things. Still, I take time to look around; in the beauty and fragileness of spring there's hope.

Sitting on the porch, I lean back against the farmhouse wall. Maggie sits next to me enjoying the return of fly-snapping season. The sun is warm and I remove my jacket. From my pocket I also remove the letter Chris gave to her sister. For two weeks I've had the letter, and I find myself reading it at least once a day.

The note consists of two pieces of folded paper written in Chris's small, almost perfect print. The paper is light blue with clusters of daffodils and tulips in the upper left corner of each page.

My dear friend: I think of you often. These thoughts, and our phone calls, get me through each day. When it's quiet and I think of you, I know I've been blessed in spite of everything.

It's true, I did leave you holding an emotional sack when I returned to Denver. I just didn't know how to say good-bye to you, Buddie. So I decided there wouldn't be any good-byes. I guess I should've consulted you, but I had no road map for this one. In this case, previous experience wasn't very helpful.

I'm not going to rehash the feelings we have for each other — or the could-have-beens, should-have-beens. It's all there, on permanent file in your heart — and mine. Whenever you need me, search for me in a memory — and I'll be there laughing with you, holding your hand and giving you hell just like I always did.

Please take care of Maggie. Give her a hug and a scratch behind the ears for me.

I'm still not saying good-bye, Buddie. Stubborn to the last. And I only ask one thing of you. In your heart, please don't ever say good-bye to me.

Love always, Chris.

P.S. Enclosed is a photograph I knew you'd want to keep. Remember? You, me and Kate on New Year's Eve? Like Kate said, "three foxy looking women!"

A pick-up truck pulls into the driveway next to the barn. Carefully, I place the letter back into its envelope. I meander down onto the grass. A tanned, older gentleman steps out of the truck and waves. As the owner of the farm approaches, I feel the onset of another loss I've also tried to anticipate.

"Hi, Buddie. Spring's in the air."

"Yes, Mr. Covington, it's a beautiful day."

"What's to happen with Maggie now that Chris is gone?"

"She's coming to live with me. We can both use a friend right now. I'm going to miss the farm and the horses," I say, looking toward the sun-cast field and rolling hills in the distance. "This has been a second home to me."

"You come and visit whenever you like, Buddie."

A few minutes later, Maggie's sitting on the passenger seat next to me. I pull the car out of the driveway, mentally saying good-bye to the farm. In my heart, I know I'll never be back.

* * * * *

The murmuring of voices and people's movements echo along the crowded hallways and rooms of the National Museum of Women in the Arts. As I browse through each wing, I marvel at the sculptures, paintings, photographs and drawings of regional contemporary women artists. I know why I'm here: to mark time, to acknowledge the final stretch of a long road.

The corridor before me opens into the largest of the exhibit rooms housing several collections of oil paintings. Some of the paintings encompass an entire walled section of the gallery. In the far right corner of its vast space, I finally find Chris — or what's left of her. The soft, shadowed colors of fields surrounding the farm in Vienna, the linear patterns of a large patriarchal city — its marble monuments, power and poverty. From the gentle farmlands of Virginia to the intense contrasts of Washington, D.C., Chris has recreated a dramatic vision of life — its peacefulness as well as its invasiveness.

The next canvas startles, then numbs me. It is, by far, Chris's largest work — located in the center of her exhibit. On a human level, it seems to anchor the body of her art. It's a portrait of three women painted from a Polaroid photograph now safely preserved inside an album at my apartment.

Chris stands in the center of the painting flanked by Kate to her left, myself to her right. It's not only a self-portrait, but a study of individual personalities.

A dramatic burst of light enters the canvas from the left, adding contrast and shadow lines to the strong, sharp features of Kate's face, her smile competing with that light for dominance. Kate's eyes are orange-brown, two sunsets I remember well. As the light fades across the canvas, images soften. Chris, slightly turned toward me, is laughing — the brightness of her eyes easing the frailness of her face. I'm also smiling. But it's a different kind of smile, an "I don't know about life" smile I'm seeing for the first time. Its accurateness is quietly accepted.

The three of us are held together at the shoulders — three women interlocking arms to form an intimate connection. Intimate and permanent and lasting — at least on canvas. Reality had since brought a vastly different outcome. Looking at the painting, I feel very much alone.

Moving closer to the canvas, I see it's been titled: "Three Friends Celebrate the New Year."

Several minutes pass, but I don't move from the painting. Struggling for answers I've never been able to find, I wonder how to bring closure to a part of my life that's finished, as finished as the canvas in front of me.

"It's an awesome painting, isn't it? I wish Chris were here to see it with us."

The voice behind my head resonates up and down my spine. Turning toward the source, I circle to face the same earthen eyes that had stared at me from the portrait above. Before I can say anything, two arms envelop me. Without hesitation I reach around, accepting Kate into my presence.

Kate steps back; her voice is strained. "Liz, I was devastated to hear the news. Sara Chapman called me about the exhibit. I came to pay my respects to Chris."

Reluctantly, I look up into the face of a woman

who still has the power to unnerve me. "I should've called you, Kate. Things have been a blur these past weeks."

"I'm sorry, Liz. Chris was a very special person."

"How are you?"

"Okay, I think. The last eight months have been therapeutic, to say the least. I've gotten a lot accomplished."

"Will you be in town long?"

"I've finally put things to rest in California. I'm here to stay. Starting with the summer session, I'll be teaching at the university again. Seems they missed me."

"I'm glad for you, Kate."

"No more dwelling on the past. My future's here in D.C. And that's the black and white of it."

"No rose-colored glasses?"

"I thought you might lend me a pair of yours." Kate looks up at Chris's canvas. "Chris's painting says it all, Liz. Everything you and I need to know. That some bonds can never be broken — in life or in death."

Kate's words hit me hard. The painting's not an ending, but a continuance. A continuance of memories I'll never say good-bye to.

Looking at the woman next to me, I think of other memories. "It's true, Kate. Chris's vision was always twenty-twenty. Some bonds are impossible to break."

"Will you have lunch with me, Liz?"

"Maybe."

"Maybe? You know me. I'll keep asking until you say yes."

"Yes."

Leaving the museum together, Kate and I step into the day's bright sunlight, walking a zigzagging path along the sidewalks of New York Avenue. As we fight our way through the crowds of Saturday tourists, I try to follow in back of Kate. The onrush of motor traffic adds to a frenzy that seems to make this city physically shudder in the April sunlight.

As we move toward the corner and into the street, Kate stays in front, pushing her way through the crowd. Without looking back, Kate reaches behind and takes my hand, pulling me with her into the stream of people. I follow close behind, not wanting to lose sight of Chris's vision.

A few of the publications of
THE NAIAD PRESS, INC.
P.O. Box 10543 • Tallahassee, Florida 32302
Phone (904) 539-5965
Toll-Free Order Number: 1-800-533-1973
Mail orders welcome. Please include 15% postage.

CABIN FEVER by Carol Schmidt. 256 pp. Sizzling suspense
and passion. ISBN 1-56280-089-1 $10.95

THERE WILL BE NO GOODBYES by Laura DeHart Young. 192
pp. Romantic love, strength, and friendship. ISBN 1-56280-103-1 10.95

FAULTLINE by Sheila Ortiz Taylor. 144 pp. Joyous comic
lesbian novel. ISBN 1-56280-108-2 9.95

OPEN HOUSE by Pat Welch. 176 pp. P.I. Helen Black's fourth
case. ISBN 1-56280-102-3 10.95

ONCE MORE WITH FEELING by Peggy J. Herring. 240 pp.
Lighthearted, loving romantic adventure. ISBN 1-56280-089-2 10.95

FOREVER by Evelyn Kennedy. 224 pp. Passionate romance — love
overcoming all obstacles. ISBN 1-56280-094-9 10.95

WHISPERS by Kris Bruyer. 176 pp. Romantic ghost story
ISBN 1-56280-082-5 10.95

NIGHT SONGS by Penny Mickelbury. 224 pp. A Gianna
Maglione Mystery. Second in a series. ISBN 1-56280-097-3 10.95

GETTING TO THE POINT by Teresa Stores. 256 pp. Classic
southern Lesbian novel. ISBN 1-56280-100-7 10.95

PAINTED MOON by Karin Kallmaker. 224 pp. Delicious
Kallmaker romance. ISBN 1-56280-075-2 9.95

THE MYSTERIOUS NAIAD edited by Katherine V. Forrest &
Barbara Grier. 320 pp. Love stories by Naiad Press authors.
ISBN 1-56280-074-4 14.95

DAUGHTERS OF A CORAL DAWN by Katherine V. Forrest.
240 pp. Tenth Anniversay Edition. ISBN 1-56280-104-X 10.95

BODY GUARD by Claire McNab. 208 pp. A Carol Ashton Mystery.
6th in a series. ISBN 1-56280-073-6 9.95

CACTUS LOVE by Lee Lynch. 192 pp. Stories by the beloved
storyteller. ISBN 1-56280-071-X 9.95

SECOND GUESS by Rose Beecham. 216 pp. An Amanda Valentine
Mystery. 2nd in a series. ISBN 1-56280-069-8 9.95

THE SURE THING by Melissa Hartman. 208 pp. L.A. earthquake
romance.   ISBN 1-56280-078-7   9.95

A RAGE OF MAIDENS by Lauren Wright Douglas. 240 pp. A
Caitlin Reece Mystery. 6th in a series.   ISBN 1-56280-068-X   9.95

TRIPLE EXPOSURE by Jackie Calhoun. 224 pp. Romantic drama
involving many characters.   ISBN 1-56280-067-1   9.95

UP, UP AND AWAY by Catherine Ennis. 192 pp. Delightful
romance.   ISBN 1-56280-065-5   9.95

PERSONAL ADS by Robbi Sommers. 176 pp. Sizzling short
stories.   ISBN 1-56280-059-0   9.95

FLASHPOINT by Katherine V. Forrest. 256 pp. Lesbian
blockbuster!   ISBN 1-56280-043-4   22.95

CROSSWORDS by Penny Sumner. 256 pp. 2nd Victoria Cross
Mystery.   ISBN 1-56280-064-7   9.95

SWEET CHERRY WINE by Carol Schmidt. 224 pp. A novel of
suspense.   ISBN 1-56280-063-9   9.95

CERTAIN SMILES by Dorothy Tell. 160 pp. Erotic short stories.
                                             ISBN 1-56280-066-3   9.95

EDITED OUT by Lisa Haddock. 224 pp. 1st Carmen Ramirez
Mystery.   ISBN 1-56280-077-9   9.95

WEDNESDAY NIGHTS by Camarin Grae. 288 pp. Sexy
adventure.   ISBN 1-56280-060-4   10.95

SMOKEY O by Celia Cohen. 176 pp. Relationships on the
playing field.   ISBN 1-56280-057-4   9.95

KATHLEEN O'DONALD by Penny Hayes. 256 pp. Rose and
Kathleen find each other and employment in 1909 NYC.
                                             ISBN 1-56280-070-1   9.95

STAYING HOME by Elisabeth Nonas. 256 pp. Molly and Alix
want a baby . . . or do they?   ISBN 1-56280-076-0   10.95

TRUE LOVE by Jennifer Fulton. 240 pp. Six lesbians searching
for love in all the "right" places.   ISBN 1-56280-035-3   9.95

GARDENIAS WHERE THERE ARE NONE by Molleen Zanger.
176 pp. Why is Melanie inextricably drawn to the old house?
                                             ISBN 1-56280-056-6   9.95

KEEPING SECRETS by Penny Mickelbury. 208 pp. A Gianna
Maglione Mystery. First in a series.   ISBN 1-56280-052-3   9.95

THE ROMANTIC NAIAD edited by Katherine V. Forrest &
Barbara Grier. 336 pp. Love stories by Naiad Press authors.
                                             ISBN 1-56280-054-X   14.95

UNDER MY SKIN by Jaye Maiman. 336 pp. A Robin Miller
mystery. 3rd in a series.   ISBN 1-56280-049-3.   10.95

STAY TOONED by Rhonda Dicksion. 144 pp. Cartoons — 1st
collection since *Lesbian Survival Manual.*   ISBN 1-56280-045-0   9.95

CAR POOL by Karin Kallmaker. 272pp. Lesbians on wheels
and then some!   ISBN 1-56280-048-5   9.95

NOT TELLING MOTHER: STORIES FROM A LIFE by Diane
Salvatore. 176 pp. Her 3rd novel.   ISBN 1-56280-044-2   9.95

GOBLIN MARKET by Lauren Wright Douglas. 240pp. A Caitlin
Reece Mystery. 5th in a series.   ISBN 1-56280-047-7   10.95

LONG GOODBYES by Nikki Baker. 256 pp. A Virginia Kelly
mystery. 3rd in a series.   ISBN 1-56280-042-6   9.95

FRIENDS AND LOVERS by Jackie Calhoun. 224 pp. Mid-western
Lesbian lives and loves.   ISBN 1-56280-041-8   10.95

THE CAT CAME BACK by Hilary Mullins. 208 pp. Highly
praised Lesbian novel.   ISBN 1-56280-040-X   9.95

BEHIND CLOSED DOORS by Robbi Sommers. 192 pp. Hot,
erotic short stories.   ISBN 1-56280-039-6   9.95

CLAIRE OF THE MOON by Nicole Conn. 192 pp. See the
movie — read the book!   ISBN 1-56280-038-8   10.95

SILENT HEART by Claire McNab. 192 pp. Exotic Lesbian
romance.   ISBN 1-56280-036-1   10.95

HAPPY ENDINGS by Kate Brandt. 272 pp. Intimate conversations
with Lesbian authors.   ISBN 1-56280-050-7   10.95

THE SPY IN QUESTION by Amanda Kyle Williams. 256 pp.
4th Madison McGuire.   ISBN 1-56280-037-X   9.95

SAVING GRACE by Jennifer Fulton. 240 pp. Adventure and
romantic entanglement.   ISBN 1-56280-051-5   9.95

THE YEAR SEVEN by Molleen Zanger. 208 pp. Women surviving
in a new world.   ISBN 1-56280-034-5   9.95

CURIOUS WINE by Katherine V. Forrest. 176 pp. Tenth Anniver-
sary Edition. The most popular contemporary Lesbian love story.
      ISBN 1-56280-053-1   10.95
      Audio Book (2 cassettes)   ISBN 1-56280-105-8   16.95

CHAUTAUQUA by Catherine Ennis. 192 pp. Exciting, romantic
adventure.   ISBN 1-56280-032-9   9.95

A PROPER BURIAL by Pat Welch. 192 pp. A Helen Black
mystery. 3rd in a series.   ISBN 1-56280-033-7   9.95

SILVERLAKE HEAT: A Novel of Suspense by Carol Schmidt.
240 pp. Rhonda is as hot as Laney's dreams.   ISBN 1-56280-031-0   9.95

LOVE, ZENA BETH by Diane Salvatore. 224 pp. The most talked
about lesbian novel of the nineties!   ISBN 1-56280-030-2   10.95

A DOORYARD FULL OF FLOWERS by Isabel Miller. 160 pp.
Stories incl. 2 sequels to *Patience and Sarah.*   ISBN 1-56280-029-9   9.95

MURDER BY TRADITION by Katherine V. Forrest. 288 pp. A
Kate Delafield Mystery. 4th in a series.   ISBN 1-56280-002-7   9.95

THE EROTIC NAIAD edited by Katherine V. Forrest & Barbara
Grier. 224 pp. Love stories by Naiad Press authors.
ISBN 1-56280-026-4   13.95

DEAD CERTAIN by Claire McNab. 224 pp. A Carol Ashton
mystery. 5th in a series.   ISBN 1-56280-027-2   9.95

CRAZY FOR LOVING by Jaye Maiman. 320 pp. A Robin Miller
mystery. 2nd in a series.   ISBN 1-56280-025-6   9.95

STONEHURST by Barbara Johnson. 176 pp. Passionate regency
romance.   ISBN 1-56280-024-8   9.95

INTRODUCING AMANDA VALENTINE by Rose Beecham.
256 pp. An Amanda Valentine Mystery. First in a series.
ISBN 1-56280-021-3   9.95

UNCERTAIN COMPANIONS by Robbi Sommers. 204 pp.
Steamy, erotic novel.   ISBN 1-56280-017-5   9.95

A TIGER'S HEART by Lauren W. Douglas. 240 pp. A Caitlin
Reece mystery. 4th in a series.   ISBN 1-56280-018-3   9.95

PAPERBACK ROMANCE by Karin Kallmaker. 256 pp. A
delicious romance.   ISBN 1-56280-019-1   9.95

MORTON RIVER VALLEY by Lee Lynch. 304 pp. Lee Lynch
at her best!   ISBN 1-56280-016-7   9.95

THE LAVENDER HOUSE MURDER by Nikki Baker. 224 pp.
A Virginia Kelly Mystery. 2nd in a series.   ISBN 1-56280-012-4   9.95

PASSION BAY by Jennifer Fulton. 224 pp. Passionate romance,
virgin beaches, tropical skies.   ISBN 1-56280-028-0   10.95

STICKS AND STONES by Jackie Calhoun. 208 pp. Contemporary
lesbian lives and loves.   ISBN 1-56280-020-5   9.95
Audio Book (2 cassettes)   ISBN 1-56280-106-6   16.95

DELIA IRONFOOT by Jeane Harris. 192 pp. Adventure for Delia
and Beth in the Utah mountains.   ISBN 1-56280-014-0   9.95

UNDER THE SOUTHERN CROSS by Claire McNab. 192 pp.
Romantic nights Down Under.   ISBN 1-56280-011-6   9.95

GRASSY FLATS by Penny Hayes. 256 pp. Lesbian romance in
the '30s.   ISBN 1-56280-010-8   9.95

A SINGULAR SPY by Amanda K. Williams. 192 pp. 3rd
Madison McGuire.   ISBN 1-56280-008-6   8.95

THE END OF APRIL by Penny Sumner. 240 pp. A Victoria
Cross mystery. First in a series.   ISBN 1-56280-007-8   8.95

HOUSTON TOWN by Deborah Powell. 208 pp. A Hollis
Carpenter mystery.   ISBN 1-56280-006-X   8.95

KISS AND TELL by Robbi Sommers. 192 pp. Scorching stories
by the author of *Pleasures*.   ISBN 1-56280-005-1   10.95

STILL WATERS by Pat Welch. 208 pp. A Helen Black mystery.
2nd in a series.   ISBN 0-941483-97-5   9.95

TO LOVE AGAIN by Evelyn Kennedy. 208 pp. Wildly romantic
love story.   ISBN 0-941483-85-1   9.95

IN THE GAME by Nikki Baker. 192 pp. A Virginia Kelly
mystery. First in a series.   ISBN 1-56280-004-3   9.95

AVALON by Mary Jane Jones. 256 pp. A Lesbian Arthurian
romance.   ISBN 0-941483-96-7   9.95

STRANDED by Camarin Grae. 320 pp. Entertaining, riveting
adventure.   ISBN 0-941483-99-1   9.95

THE DAUGHTERS OF ARTEMIS by Lauren Wright Douglas.
240 pp. A Caitlin Reece mystery. 3rd in a series.
                                                 ISBN 0-941483-95-9   9.95

CLEARWATER by Catherine Ennis. 176 pp. Romantic secrets
of a small Louisiana town.   ISBN 0-941483-65-7   8.95

THE HALLELUJAH MURDERS by Dorothy Tell. 176 pp. A
Poppy Dillworth mystery. 2nd in a series.   ISBN 0-941483-88-6   8.95

SECOND CHANCE by Jackie Calhoun. 256 pp. Contemporary
Lesbian lives and loves.   ISBN 0-941483-93-2   9.95

BENEDICTION by Diane Salvatore. 272 pp. Striking, contemporary romantic novel.   ISBN 0-941483-90-8   9.95

BLACK IRIS by Jeane Harris. 192 pp. Caroline's hidden past . . .
                                                 ISBN 0-941483-68-1   8.95

TOUCHWOOD by Karin Kallmaker. 240 pp. Loving, May/
December romance.   ISBN 0-941483-76-2   9.95

COP OUT by Claire McNab. 208 pp. A Carol Ashton mystery.
4th in a series.   ISBN 0-941483-84-3   9.95

THE BEVERLY MALIBU by Katherine V. Forrest. 288 pp. A
Kate Delafield Mystery. 3rd in a series.   ISBN 0-941483-48-7   10.95

THAT OLD STUDEBAKER by Lee Lynch. 272 pp. Andy's affair
with Regina and her attachment to her beloved car.
                                                 ISBN 0-941483-82-7   9.95

PASSION'S LEGACY by Lori Paige. 224 pp. Sarah is swept into
the arms of Augusta Pym in this delightful historical romance.
                                                 ISBN 0-941483-81-9   8.95

These are just a few of the many Naiad Press titles — we are the oldest and
largest lesbian/feminist publishing company in the world. Please request a
complete catalog. We offer personal service; we encourage and welcome
direct mail orders from individuals who have limited access to bookstores
carrying our publications.